17 Resentment Court

DAVID W. STOESZ

Contents

In a pagoda gazebo

I CAME TO PLANKTON to get away from a woman. A woman with a dirty mind, a heart like a roller-coaster accident, and a husband. One time she drew five stars on my cock with a Sharpie. After I went limp they looked like asterisks. When she left, I was going to throw myself into the Ohio River. Instead, a bus ran over my foot, and I got a bunch of insurance money and left for Plankton.

Things went bad for her, too, but not because she was heartbroken or anything. Her husband found out. I agreed to meet him, and offered to let him hit me in the face. I didn't know he would be so good at hitting. My right eyeball was still bloody when I arrived in Plankton. That might have explained why people weren't friendly. I doubt it though.

Plankton is on the ocean. It rises like a pinch of flesh between a bay with jaggedy edges and a lake shaped like the dot of a question mark. The bay is called Hello Bay and the lake is called What Lake. It rains a lot.

My cab from the airport was shuttered like a confessional by a storm on the windows. The cab said "Plankton Welcomes the Pope" on the side. The Pope had just been there.

"You want to hear something funny?" I asked the driver. He didn't look like he wanted to hear something funny. "Your sign says, welcome to the Pope, and my name is Pope." He didn't react. Which was fine. But there's something called "making an effort." There's also something called "meet me halfway, dickhole." Not for this crowd though. Talk to them for more than three seconds and it's like you're soliciting a blow job.

Frank Boise was probably good at hitting. He was a former college football star and still had the build to match. To me, he was a floating array of soft-tissue targets. Nuts, eyeballs, underarms. He'd probably take me though, to be honest.

When I saw his ad—INVESTIGATOR SEEKS OPERATIVE—I'd had enough of limping around town and trying to chat with people who edged away from my bloody eyeball. Whatever an operative was, it couldn't possibly be more boring than tapping at a keyboard and looking at a screen. That's what I did at the job I had before I came to Plankton.

Boise's office was in Trapper's Yard, Plankton's "historical" district, a few old brick buildings huddled on streets of re-created cobblestone at the edge of Hello Bay. Boise was on the second floor of a building with a lion's head over the door and old-timey doodads in the eaves. His receptionist wore a lavender dress and armor of absolute disinterest.

I took a brochure about Zion's Gate Alarm System from a little stand on her desk. It casts an unbroken net of electric current around your home. Anyone breaking this net will trigger a siren and a call to the dispatcher. I was lost in the pixelated breasts of the stock-photography wife when Boise appeared in the doorway and summoned me into his office with a blank smile aimed over my shoulder.

He had a mustache, a little poof of an Afro, arms like tugboat lines sprawled across his oak desk, and championship clippings yellowing on the wall behind him. He handed me his card, glanced at the threadbare details of my job history, wrote a few things down. Then he told me what he wanted me to do.

"There's a guy named Maurice. We need to get him a message, but he doesn't have an address. You'll probably find him at Yick Fung Overlook. You know where that is?" I did. It's a park built into a hill in Chinatown. "You'll might catch him if you go there now."

He pushed two envelopes across the desk. One envelope said *M* and the other said *You.* "Give this one to Maurice, and keep this one. There's twenty bucks in there. Wait, did I say twenty? I meant *thirty.* Yours free and clear." He smiled again. "Come back after you see him and I'll give you another thirty. I may ask you some questions about what you see, so keep your peepers skinned. You're actually going to be undercover." He widened his eyes a little at the word. What a thrill for the kid, undercover as a gullible dipshit. I noticed the fittings on Boise's windows were stamped with the Zion's Gate logo: a fist holding a bolt of lightning. Why a fist? Why not a gate?

Boise produced a red cowboy hat and put it on the desk. "Also, I want you to wear this when you go." He smiled weakly out the window to express how incidental this detail was.

"Do you have any questions?"

I told him I didn't, since he obviously wasn't going to tell me anything.

"I'd tell you more, but then I'd have to kill you." He laughed as if he'd just made that up. Then he gave me a couple of pens that said *Frank Boise* on the side. "These are good pens. I'll give you a free business tip: never put your name on cheap shit."

He was right about the pens. They turned out to be excellent.

Boise was getting bored. "This is just a one-time thing for now," he said, drawing his performance to a close, "but I'm sure there'll be more stuff for you later."

More stuff. I was already leaving with two envelopes, a cowboy hat, a business card, some truly excellent pens, and a brochure describing his security system. Outside, I put on the cowboy hat and opened the envelope for Maurice. It had a piece of paper that said "Reindeer."

Yick Fung Overlook was a 20-minute limp to the south. The cops tolerated drug activity there to keep it out of other parts of town. It was named for a businessman who built hospitals and paid for school orchestras. I'd read the plaque when I'd been there to buy weed.

I bet if Yick Fung were still around he'd have been pissed. "Look, white man," he'd say, "we built your railroads. We did your laundry. I even put that clarinet in your daughter's mouth. Take your drug dealers back."

A path zigzagged to the top of the park, where there was a gazebo shaped like a pagoda. It was too early for the guys who sold hard drugs, but not for the woman who'd sold me weed before. She was sitting on a table inside the pagoda gazebo.

"Got a cigarette?" she asked without looking up. She was already smoking one. She wore a jean jacket and a second jean jacket on top of it with the sleeves cut off. I shook out four cigarettes and put them on her table.

"You lookin'?" She nestled further into her jean jackets. She was doing a great impression of someone not excited to see me. Maybe she didn't like my hat. Still, she was at that moment my second-best friend in town, right after Boise. And I was lookin', having smoked my whole stash on marathon limps around Plankton. I exchanged the envelope of cash from Boise for a plastic bag. She managed the entire transaction without moving anything other than her wrist.

I leaned against a post and lit my own cigarette and helped her blow smoke toward the airport, which you can almost see from the top of Yick Fung.

"Say," I ventured after a minute, "do you know a guy named Maurice?"

"No."

"You don't know a single person named Maurice?"

"What did I just say?"

"Not even in the past? Like maybe a Maurice in your kindergarten class?"

"That's stupid."

I leaned and smoked some more. "So is it a pretty good day for airplanes?"

She finally looked at me. "What?"

"Nothing. Just shooting the shit. You ever do that?"

"Do what?"

"Talk about bullshit with someone to pass the time."

"Why?"

"Yeah, no reason, I guess. Well, it sure was nice catching up with you."

She turned her attention back to the horizon.

Descending, I spotted a foot sticking out of a planter. It belonged to Ed Cranberry, though I didn't know that yet.

I limped on by. Someone else would spot the foot. I'm sure they'd feel real important when they called it in. I wasn't so desperate for a conversation that I wanted one with the cops.

The news said the cause of death was poisoning. He had also been stabbed. And apparently shot with a pellet gun. No word on if he'd been tickled. Then he was dumped in a cement planter on Yick Fung Overlook. A Parks employee had found him not long after I saw his foot. It was news for a day, then nothing. No angry vows by the police to track down the killer, no interviews with his colleagues about what a great guy he was. Plankton was apparently unimpressed. Also, no mention of Boise, and no clue as to why he'd chuck a limping out-of-towner into a half-assed setup job.

Ed Cranberry had a daughter. It wasn't hard to find her number. "Hello, Helen Cranberry?" I said when she answered. "I'm sorry to call you at a time like this. I'm investigating your dad's death. My name is Frank Boise."

Helen Cranberry

ESENTMENT COURT IS a row of connected units, each with its own little fenced-in square of brown grass. A little boy in front of unit sixteen watched me walk up to unit seventeen.

"Are you a social worker?" he asked over the fence.

"No," I said, making my hand into a gun. "I kill social workers."

I knocked on the door and Helen Cranberry opened it. I said, "Thank you for taking the time for this," and handed her Frank Boise's card.

We sat down in her crappy living room. She answered my questions and I wrote down what she said in a little notebook with one of my Frank Boise pens.

"Dad was on sabbatical. That was part of the problem. He wasn't busy enough."

"He get into trouble?"

"No." She looked down. "I mean, other than with the group."

"The group?"

She swallowed. "Do we have to pretend you don't know?"

I tried to think of a good answer to that. "Of course not." I wrote *The group* in smooth, silky lines.

She said she didn't know how he'd spent the last week of his life. "When I got pregnant with Hector," she said, nodding at an unplanned baby asleep by a rack of liquor, "he took it badly, and we weren't talking much at the end."

"How long have you lived here, Ms. Cranberry?"

"You mean why do I live in a dump when my parents have money?"

"I'm sorry if—"

"No, it's fine. Things aren't great with my mom, either. She wasn't too good even before Dad died. The divorce fucked her up."

"Did your dad have friends at the university?"

"Not really. Except Sandbag."

"Sandbag?"

"Sandy Sandbag." Helen shifted on the sofa. "The chair of his department. Stood by him after everyone else had concluded he was an asshole."

"He wasn't popular?"

"He did things his own way."

I wrote *Was an asshole* and clicked my Frank Boise pen closed. "What else can you tell me about him?"

"He was . . . a dork." She wiped her eyes on her sleeve. "He had his own little names for everything. When we biked around What Lake, there was a part where we always went off the path and rode through the trees. He called it the 'Interlude of Bumpiness.' When I cleaned out his apartment I found a map of Plankton I drew when I was ten. With his names for all the places . . ." She covered her face.

"Can I get you . . .?"

She shook her head and waved me off.

I told her I was sorry and stood up.

Back outside, the little boy was still standing in front of unit sixteen. He held out a piece of paper. "*Rick Fernmancer,*" it said in careful letters. "He's a social worker," the boy said. "I want you to kill him."

"What's your name?"

"Noah."

"People call you No?" He shook his head. "You got any money, No?"

He rummaged in his pocket and came out with a five-dollar bill. I took it from him and snapped it. A piece of lint arced over his head. "I'll be honest with you, No. This isn't a lot of money. But I'll see what I can do." I put the money and the piece of paper that said *Rick Fernmancer* in my pocket with the Boise card I'd taken back from Helen Cranberry's coffee table while she was busy crying. Noah was still watching as I rounded the corner at the end of the row of brown squares of grass.

Some complaints and a burglary

I WROTE THE TOP four things I hated about Plankton on an index card and pinned it to the wall.

1. Everyone's faces
2. Everyone's clothes
3. My neighbors

Once when I was out in the courtyard with a vodka lemonade and a cigarette, I was informed by a lady still in her office clothes that it was a no-smoking area. I told her I'd just finish this one. She didn't move. She said it was a no-smoking-anytime area. I told her it would be pretty funny if something happened to her dog. She covered her mouth with her hands and rushed off. Some people have no sense of humor.

4. Frank Boise

That asshole. What was supposed to have happened at Yick Fung Overlook? My conversation with Helen Cranberry told me nothing. I decided to break into his office. He was practically inviting me in with that Zion's Gate system. The way it works is that pairs of magnets go on all your windows and doors, and if anything opens, the magnets are separated and the circuit is broken and the alarm goes off. Any decent burglar can find a way to go through the window without opening it.

Not that I'm a burglar. Sure, I used to do the kind of crazy stuff all kids do. Drinking, throwing rocks, the occasional break-in. And that did eventually lead to being part of what you might technically call a "burglary ring." But that's a misleading term.

Boise's office was on the second floor, with a window that faced an alley. The building is made with historically important lumpy bricks. Walking through a park one day, I saw an old water tower with the same kind of lumpy bricks. With a little practice,

I could climb it to about the height of Boise's window in thirty seconds. It didn't even hurt my foot that much.

"Excuse me!" A voice from below. An upturned face under a black cap. Security guy. "You can't be up there!"

"OK, I guess I'll just drop my ass into your face then. How would that be? Would that be pretty neat?"

He stepped back sharply and put his hand on his belt.

"No, no, don't call for backup, Der Kommissar. I'm coming down. Just messing with you. No harm, eh?"

I offered to shake his hand to show that everything was cool, but no go. Another cold fish.

I got a bike at a thrift store and some bike crap to help me blend in. Helmet, reflective vest, stretchy pants with a cradle for your balls. Plankton is all about exercise clothes. They want to be ready to take off running in the opposite direction in case you try to talk to them.

The bike stuff was my first outfit for the Boise job. For my second one, I'd dress like one of the men who fill the bars in Trapper's Yard: jeans, a T-shirt, ball cap. In the thrift-store changing room, I looked like anyone or no one.

The night of the job, I put on my bike suit and packed the other clothes in a messenger bag, along with a glass cutter, a crowbar, thin cotton gloves, and a halogen penlight. The glass cutter was Japanese, with a pistol grip and eight cams in the axle bore of the cutting wheel. I was going to hate to lose it to the trash when I was done with it. I also had a small blanket to put over the windowpane. If you do it right, the blanket falls in with the glass and muffles the sound.

I learned that trick doing jobs with my friends. We started breaking into places as a way to stay out of trouble after we accidentally burned the school down one night. It wasn't our fault. Banh had brought his idiot cousin along, and he started a fire in a garbage can. The first actual job we did was an electronics store. It was easy. It had the same kind of security system as the school. We loaded my dad's station wagon and were gone in five minutes. We made a list of other places that had that system and hit them all.

I biked to Trapper's Yard and locked up in front of a bookstore three blocks from Boise's office. It was crowded with other bikes. Biking to a reading is a wild night for a Planktonite.

I headed for the back door of a bar called Brad's Blazer that I'd scouted out the day before. It was propped open for ventilation. In the men's room, I put on the jeans and T-shirt over my spandex, swapped my helmet for the ball cap, and changed into sneakers. The messenger bag was the only thing I now shared with the bicyclist look, so I turned it inside out. In place of a bike dork stood a forgettable white man. White enough anyway, if I angled the brim of my cap over my face.

I left Brad's Blazer having been seen only by a man swaying in front of a urinal. Three blocks later I stood at the mouth of Boise's alley on a side street off the main strip. A plastic bag in a tree had filled with rain. The shadow of a leaf inside the bag sloshed back and forth on the sidewalk.

I unlocked the wheels of a dumpster and pushed my back against it until it was under Boise's window, then walked around the block to make sure the racket hadn't attracted attention. I got on top of the dumpster and started climbing. *Never hurry, never rest* was one of the principles of burglary I wrote down for the benefit of the other Riders. That's what my friends and I called ourselves. It started as a drunken joke and stuck. It was short for "The Really Invincible Riders."

Boise's brick wall was even lumpier than the water tower in the park. Total time to the window was about twenty seconds. I had to cut the pane with one hand. I needed the other to hold onto the ledge, so I couldn't do the trick with the blanket. I scored out the pane and pushed with the back of my hand. Traffic noise from the strip washed away the tinkle of the glass. I used my bag to cover the razor edge left in the window frame and threw my bad leg into Boise's office.

It's not that I thought I was better than the other Riders when I suggested a few principles of burglary I thought we could agree on. But that's how they took it. "Tell us more, Professor Pope!"

Assholes.

I put on the cotton gloves, pushed the power button on Boise's computer, and applied my crowbar to his filing cabinet under the watchful eye of a little golden man on a trophy. *Q, R, S . . . Smith, Pope.* My file held a single sheet of Zion's Gate stationery. I read it with the penlight in my mouth:

POPE SMITH

Skinny as a stork

Dumb as a rock

Leaps for cash

A gazelle!

A bum on a baloney sandwich!

Under that was the date of my job interview and the initials *FB*. I put it back and flipped through the rest of the files. Nothing but legalese tales of divorce and surveillance. I turned back to the computer. It wanted a password. I turned it off. I scooped a handful of his excellent pens into my messenger bag.

I saw something. Something bad. I was being watched. Not the man on the trophy. A red dot in a plastic casing mounted in the shadow between two bookcases. It blinked when I moved. So Boise knew Zion's Gate was shit and had a second system. About three minutes had passed since my entry. I sprinted to the window, dangled from the ledge, and dropped to the dumpster.

Ten more seconds to exit the alley and round the corner to the main drag, where I fell in behind a pack of guys dressed like me. Five steps in, flashing lights hit the back of my neck. I zigzagged through the crowd to the second bar I'd scouted out, the Big Ol' Rooster.

I sat at the bar, ordered a beer, and averted my bloody eyeball from the bartender. There was a soccer match on TV. A team in mustard and a team in black and red. I got up, put a ten under my glass, and hit the men's room stall. I thought of the time I fucked the married woman in a stall while she braced herself on the handicap railing. The memory was laced with razor. I stripped to my bicycle costume, changed my shoes, and put the helmet back on. I stuffed the clothes I didn't need anymore into my messenger bag, which was now turned right-side-in again. Outside the Big Ol' Rooster, my bicycle shoes sounded like high heels on the pavement.

Back home, I made toast and ate it with the lights out.

The tiers of a clown

OUR LAST MEETING had ended with sobbing. Helen Cranberry wasn't sobbing now. She was cradling the elbow of her smoking arm and squinting at my questions.

Considering what I'd learned from the burglary—only that my opponent considered himself a satirical poet—I'd decided to track Helen to her job at East Sea Sushi. We were on the roof of a parking garage downtown. The restaurant staff smoked there. The restaurant itself was on the top floor of a department store across the street, connected to the garage by a sky bridge.

"I don't remember who you said hired you."

"The teacher's union at the university. They're afraid more professors are going to be killed."

A couple of guys in head scarves in the window of East Sea Sushi were working their shoulders over something behind the sushi bar. In the other direction, a slice of Hello Bay glimmered between gray buildings.

"Well, I don't have any more time for you. I gotta go set up." She was wearing her black-and-whites and an apron with a crane on it.

"Can we keep talking though? I can fold napkins."

She stubbed her cigarette out on the ledge and dropped it into a can that had once held baby bamboo. "Tatsu's out catering, so I guess. But you have to get out before we open. And don't touch the napkins."

I followed her over the sky bridge, taking notes with a Boise pen.

"Tatsu's the boss?"

"The Commander, the Overlord, the Little Senator."

"Where's the catering gig?"

"My mom's house, actually."

Her mom's house? "And you're not invited?"

"Mom being fancy with the ladies from the board, plus Tatsu? No thanks." Helen swiped an ID badge on a pad by the restaurant's service entrance. The door pulled itself closed behind us and the ambient noise shifted into a lower octave. She clocked in on a point-of-sale machine and pulled a shrink-wrapped wad of washcloths from a shelf.

"Are you surprised she can have a party so soon after your dad's death?"

"I'm not her therapist." She unwrapped the washcloths and dumped them in one side of a double sink. A block of shrimp was defrosting under a dribble of water in the other half of the sink. She soaked the washcloths with hot water, then returned the faucet to its dribble over the shrimp.

"So this is how you make those hot cloths."

She was wringing out the cloths and rolling them into little logs. "*Oshibori*. Yes."

"I could help you do that."

"No. It would take too long to teach you." She was stacking them in rows in a plastic tub. I bet it would feel great to wipe your ass with one of those things. One of the head-scarf men from the window came in and poked at the block of shrimp with a stubby finger.

"Hey, tell your crew, we got two six-tops soon as the doors open." He squatted in front of a fridge, his back to Helen.

"They're not my crew."

"Don't fuck it up!"

Helen didn't look up as he left spanking a slab of tuna.

"Charming fellow," I said.

"He's running for the position of Tatsu Junior. OK, so what other important details do you need to catch this professor killer?"

I smiled at her misunderstanding of an investigator's job. "Well, I'm just trying to get the bigger picture here. Could you tell me more about your parents' divorce?"

She looked at the ceiling, then at the shrimp in the sink.

"Dad left with his clothes and a cocktail shaker. Started living in a rental like a college kid. Getting back to basics, he said. He'd slink back when Mom wasn't home to snag things that turned out to be more basic than he thought. The blender, the coffee maker, some of his books, his gun. The house was basically a storage unit to him. Mom changed the locks and cried for three days."

"Did he have someone else?"

"Don't know. We weren't talking at the end."

"Wasn't he happy to have a grandson?"

"When I got pregnant it was like an insult to his good taste. He wasn't the type to be swept up in babies."

She snapped a lid on her tub of *oshibori* and put it on the bottom shelf of a refrigerator.

"Why did you put those in there?"

"They go bad. Is that an angle professor killers would use?"

I smiled my professional smile. "OK, I'll leave you alone, Ms. Cranberry. Good luck with Tatsu Junior tonight. Want a pen?" Waitresses always need pens. She took it but didn't invite me to call her Helen.

I dreamed of a tree that led through the ceiling to a city that turned out to be an elaborate stage set. In the morning I jerked off in the shower to the Mexican mail lady. She has long messy hair and angry eyes. I imagined her thighs straddling my face. My hair was still wet when I passed her on my way out the door, the semen her image had called forth flowing in a pipe under our feet to Hello Bay.

It was a twenty-minute bike ride from my apartment to my next stop, the top of King's Crown, where Mayfern Cranberry lived. It was steep as shit. I stopped a few blocks away from the house to sit under somebody's perfect eucalyptus and did some Biz Yoga breathing.

I took out the clean white shirt I had folded up in my bag. I wanted to look plausible as Frank Boise,

Investigator. A couple of kids appeared at the edge of a semicircle of fallen eucalyptus blossoms to gape at me pulling my stretchy bike shirt over my head.

"You got a mommy?" I asked them. They nodded, very solemn. "Well, my mommy's dead. So how about you fuck off?"

They scattered like birds.

The Cranberry residence sneered down at the street from atop a three-tiered garden with stone steps snaking through it. The house was boxy and white and had a wall of frosted glass that wrapped around a corner and probably glowed like a Chinese lantern at night. I let the cast-iron knocker drop. It looked heavy but probably didn't weigh more than three hundred pounds.

Mayfern Cranberry was short, in a plain gray sweatshirt and jeans. The interior of her house gleamed behind her with the kind of clean you only get when someone else does the cleaning. Having opened the door, she seemed to have forgotten what she was doing there.

"Ms. Cranberry, Frank Boise. We talked on the phone."

I stepped forward to press my Boise card into her hands. A closer look at her eyes showed she was massively checked out.

"You're what Frank is now."

"You could put it that way. May I come in?"

She made a partial recovery and gestured to her left. In a flash of furniture polish we arrived in her living room. She stuck my card in the back pocket of her jeans, sat on the couch, and looked out the window so blankly I wondered if this really was her house. Preliminaries didn't seem to be in order.

"Ms. Cranberry, who killed your husband?"

She unbolted her gaze from the window and swung it around at me. Her eyes brimmed with too much for anything to come out.

"He killed himself." The window commanded a view of downtown. A ferry was diagonally crossing the space between buildings.

"Ms. Cranberry, given the cause of death, that seems unlikely."

"He made his choices."

I wondered what she was on. "I'll be right back. I'm going to use your toilet."

Her bathroom door opened with the smooth, heavy feeling of money well spent. She had one of those robot dog heads that lick your asshole clean mounted on a column next to the toilet. Pill bottles lined the inside of her mirror. I took one whose label

I didn't recognize—Promajil. A laptop was open on the dining room table. I sat down and looked up Promajil. For extreme anxiety. Side effects included fatigue, frequent urination, and suggestibility.

Helen called out from the living room.

"He chose those people. Frank told me about it."

"Hold that thought," I said. I sat back down and took out my notebook. "What do you mean Frank told you?"

She looked at me for the first time with something like alertness. "You should know. You said you're Frank."

I didn't have an answer to that. She went back to her first thought.

"You're what Frank is now."

"Right, that's it exactly. I'm Now Frank. New Frank. Can you do me a favor though? Can you tell me things that Old Frank told you? That will help me become one Frank again."

I gave her a moment to let that sink in.

"Paul. It was all about Paul. He was afraid of you, you know. That's what set him off."

"That makes sense. Can you remind me of Paul's last name?"

"Dowell. He works at TechCo."

Paul Dowell, TechCo. That was a nasty mouthful. I wrote it down. "And what were they planning to do? He and Paul?"

"You told me."

"Remind me."

"I'm going to sleep now."

"We're almost done."

"I'm going to lie down." She stood up.

"Just walk me out. Did Paul kill Ed?"

"I told you what happened. He chose. Just like Helen chose."

I let her walk in front of me and fished my Frank Boise card out of her back pocket. She didn't seem to notice. The card was still warm from her ass.

"What did Helen choose?"

"She took his side, you know. Ed's side."

"And what did you do about that?"

Her eyes were dimming. "I don't understand."

"I was just saying thank you. You've been a great help."

"Are you one Frank now?"

"Headed that direction, anyway." I closed the door on her stare.

I turned around to face the biggest grin I'd ever seen staring up from the second tier of the yard. It belonged to Tatsu Junior. The tuna spanker from East Sea Sushi. He was bug-eyed with ecstasy at the sight of me.

"I know you!" He regarded this as a victory of unimaginable proportions. He leaned toward me on his shovel. "What are you doing here?"

"I'm with the National Association of Organizations. You?"

Still in awe of his advantage, he indicated with his chin the Shady Lane Landscaping logo on his sweatshirt. A truck with the same logo and a Christian fish symbol on the door was parked on the street.

"Second job? You must be the hardest-working man in sushi business."

"Shit don't roll uphill, my friend."

"You may be onto something there."

I turned back to the front door and turned the knob. It wasn't locked. Mayfern was still standing there.

"What's he doing here?"

"Who?" She didn't move.

"The little guy who works at the sushi place with Helen. The one weeding your front yard."

"Are the gardeners here?" She might have been inquiring about the phases of Saturn. I gestured at the yard. Tatsu Junior was no longer there. Someone else was. With shoulders like the hull of a ship and clippers hanging at his hips, he stood like a statue by a cherry tree in the first tier. I closed the door again and ran down to him.

"Where'd the other guy go?"

"Don't know." He turned away from me and began snipping at a cherry tree.

"Come on, no kidding. Where is he?"

"Don't know." The contempt he put into these two words was pure and infinite.

"OK. Great to have met you, Skippy."

He returned to his snipping.

A tunnel in the fog

I WAS LOOKING AT surveillance photos of myself on a crime blog. They'd been taken by a camera mounted in the ceiling of Boise's office. Along with the motion detector, I'd also missed the camera.

The pictures didn't show much besides the bill of my cap and one of my cotton gloves. And the pictures were all they had. Almost like the smooth motherfucker in question had vanished in the wind.

Next, I checked the news from back home to see if my idiot former partners had been caught yet. Apparently not. And finally, the actual point of my visit: Paul Dowell, TechCo. There was no home address for Paul that I could find, but I did find out where TechCo was.

Fifteen minutes later I limped up to their lobby door. It opened with a sucking resistance. Inside, everything was white. The furniture, the fixtures, everything.

"May I help you?" The receptionist was seated behind a massive white slab.

"Yes, please. Could you tell Paul Dowell I'm here?"

A name tag said her name was Darlene. "Is he expecting you?"

"Yes he is."

"Your name?"

"Frank Boise."

Her hand paused on the number pad of the phone. "May I see some ID, please?" I lay down my Boise card. Its best days were definitely behind it. Her eyes tick-tocked from the creases in the card to my face and back to the card. She had the kind of confidence you can get only from recessed lighting.

"I don't think you're Frank Boise."

"No, Darlene," I said, "I'm a *representative* of Frank Boise. The police sent me. I'm the display manager for the embassy."

Employees dribbled by. Unlike Darlene, they looked bad. Like they were on their way to clean a garage. They had badges hanging around their necks and swiped them on a pad next to the door as they slumped through it.

"May I see some *picture* ID, please?"

"Excuse me, I have to take this." I took out my wallet and pressed it to my ear. "No, she doesn't get it. It's the old 'this isn't a picture ID' runaround. I don't know . . . yes, of course I've taken down her name." I held up a finger to Darlene and stepped away from the white slab to finish my conversation outside.

I spent the next few afternoons in a coffee shop next to TechCo. I wanted to make myself familiar to TechCo employees so I wouldn't look out of place once I made it inside.

I'd brought my laptop. It didn't work. That didn't matter. It was a prop to help me blend in. Tides of TechCo workers surged through the coffee shop and out again. Almost all men, they were dressed in diaper-shaped shorts and ratty sneakers. They carried coffee drinks around like baby bottles and said things like, "My only complaint about the veggie fried rice was . . ." and "You might want to ping Gary about that."

I sat with my tea in the corner behind my dead laptop. There was a poem taped to the screen. I passed the time trying to memorize it, tapping the keyboard in time to the words.

Now entertain conjecture of a time
When creeping murmur and the poring dark
Fills the wide vessel of the universe.

I did this for a few hours on Tuesday and Wednesday. The words wouldn't stay in my head. Thursday was foggy and I was still tapping, but slower.

From camp to camp, through the foul womb of night,
The hum of either army stilly sounds,
That the fix'd sentinels almost receive
The secret whispers of each other's watch:

"That's some battery life you have there." A woman had appeared in the coffee shop and was talking to me.

"Please, sit down."

She was already sitting down. "You haven't been plugged in all week."

My broken laptop with the poem taped to it had no power cord. I didn't think anyone would notice. "You raise an excellent point."

She had auburn hair—a dye job—and was dressed all in black. Big hips, big everything. "So what kind of power are you running that on?"

"Solar. I have a wireless unit set up outside."

"Bullshit."

"Are you an innovation builder or an obstacle salesperson? You sound like an obstacle salesperson."

"No, really. Why are you typing on a laptop that's not even on?"

I looked around. "Do you want the world to know?"

She looked me up and down. "OK, have fun." She stood up and shook my gaze from her hips as she swung them out the door. I stared into space for a minute, then packed my shit and followed her through the door and into the tunnel she'd made in the fog. I lost the thread twenty yards into the evening throng of bean-shaped men.

Memories of a beige square

FLOWERS ARE A good way to sneak into places. Way better than clipboards. You can't use a shitty little plastic tube of carnations though. You have to spend money and get something with volume. A monstrosity that hides your face and makes strangers rush to get the door for you. You can't use a florist. They could ID you. You have to buy flowers at the grocery store and make your own arrangement.

I'd taken a day off from poem memorization to follow up on Tatsu Junior, sushi chef slash landscaper. His real name was apparently Lester "Lito" Arroyo. There was an old review of East Sea Sushi online with a photo of the staff and that's what the caption said. He looked like a little kid next to the other cooks, with a kid's grin.

That's how I found myself at the Food Giant shopping for flowers. The gang of amateurs I used to run with probably would've jumped him. No work ethic. No strategy. I took home the five biggest bunches they had, cinched them at the bottom with a coat hanger, and jammed the whole circus into a preschooler-size vase from the same thrift store where I'd gotten stuff for the Boise job.

That thing wasn't going to fit through any bus doors, so I carried it to Lito's. He lived on the Hello Bay side of Plankton, in a shabby pocket of the city by the hospital. Midnight sirens kept rents low. I chose a Sunday, when he wouldn't be at work. East Sea Sushi was closed, and the fish symbol on the Shady Lane truck meant the landscapers respected the Sabbath.

I set the flowers down under the awning of a vacuum cleaner store across the street from Lito's building and shook out my arms. They were on fire. I'd only made it all the way by doing my Business Yoga breathing exercises.

The store was closed. A guy was looking in, his hands cupped on the window.

"They've got some pretty nice vacuums in there," I said.

He jerked like he'd been slapped on the neck and looked at me like I was a talking squirrel. "Yeah!" he finally managed, and scuttled off sideways.

"Ever put one on your cock?" I asked his back.

When my arms recovered, I crossed the street and made for the front door of Lito's building. There was a woman coming toward me. I held the flowers in front of my face and got to the door the same time she did. She didn't stop. I did the same dance with a dozen more passersby before scoring a hit with an old lady on her way out.

"You shouldn't have!" she said, holding the door open.

"How could I possibly resist you?" I said from behind my flowery mask.

Between rose stems, I spied a security camera in the lobby, hidden inside a tinted plastic bubble. The hallway carpet was maroon and patterned in rosettes. Dust bunnies lounged in the corners liked they owned the place. Lito's apartment was on the third floor. He didn't answer my knock.

I'm no lock picker. But I did learn the rudiments one cold Sunday afternoon when I was still with the Riders. They were in the next room getting high and watching porn. I grabbed a box of old locks we'd snagged from some guy's garage and dumped them

on the dining room table. It took about twenty minutes to get a feel for it. The pins *want* to jump into
the casing. It's what they're made to do. Since then,
I always keep a couple of paper clips and a hair pin
on me. Just in case. Lito's lock was basic. After fifteen seconds of kneeling by the door, I pulled it shut
behind me.

The blinds were half drawn on the remnants of
Lito's crummy life. A beanbag chair with a plastic
bucket mashed into it. A toy giraffe jammed into
the hollow of a cinder block. A ball of tinfoil, a jar lid
caked with dust, a tape measure, a tube of nails, a
sock. A TV on top of a milk crate. On top of the TV,
a bear-shaped plastic container of little cookies that
were also shaped like bears. A surprisingly healthy
spider plant hanging from the ceiling. A couch along
the wall that probably used to be beige. Lito was on
the couch in a yellow T-shirt and shorts. There was a
round hole in his forehead.

I cleared space on the coffee table, put the flowers
down, and said, "So I'm guessing you don't do a lot of
entertaining?" He seemed to be looking through his
half-closed eyes at the card attached to the flowers.
"Congratulations," the card said.

I didn't really know Lito, but from what I'd gath-
ered, he wasn't likable. A shrimpy little chatterbox

who probably never bought anyone a drink in his life. I guessed that if I didn't care he'd been shot in the head, no one in this city of dead fish would. And I was sick of having corpses chucked in my path. So I decided to find out who would show up next.

I opened the closet. The top magazine on a tower of magazines slithered to the ground, then they all did. I kicked them out of the way, along with a moldy slipper and a lime rind.

There was a hamper in the back of the closet. I set a tentative ass cheek on it and found it could hold my weight. I left the door open a crack for a view of Lito's corpse. The window behind him stirred with light. A strip of Scotch tape over a crack in the glass lit up like the spine of a ghost.

I did some more Business Yoga breathing to settle in. I learned that at a seminar my boss made us all go to back in my old city. Cigarettes are the one element I added to the Business Yoga system. Could I risk one there in the closet? I decided I could. It would probably improve the smell.

The guy in the seminar paced up and down in front of the words "Relax to win" projected on a screen behind him. He'd freeze his hands and face when he made a point. "In these situations, the only one who can hold you back is . . . *you*." And freeze.

Lips pursed around the final vowel, his hands a triangle pointed at the audience. I sat there wishing death upon him, and upon all people. Until we did the breathing exercises. And then it was like I'd pulled free of a narrow space that had been pressing in from all sides. My shoulders relaxed, my face relaxed, my brain unclenched.

At the end of the seminar, he mentioned a set of CDs for ninety-nine dollars. I hung back afterward to ask if he'd go lower on that price. I suggested twenty. He laughed like I was joking.

A couple weeks later, I tracked him down in the parking lot of a hotel where he was about to give another seminar. He was rummaging in his trunk.

"Hey."

He popped up straight as a stop sign.

"Interesting seminar the other day."

He looked relieved. "Oh! Well, it looks like we've made another comrade in namaste! Welcome, brother. Believe me, I get it. Once you get a taste of your own body wisdom, it's hard to stay away."

"Sure is. I also want a set of those CDs. I brought twenty dollars."

He considered the sky. "Pesky thing, money. If I could wish it away, I would. But we both have to live with it, my friend. That doesn't mean something beautiful can't arise out of it. Like a lotus emerging out of the muck. The compensation for the audio instruction is not subject to change, but that doesn't have to be an obstacle. Obstacles are just handholds we can use to climb up to the next level." He was talking a little too fast. I didn't move. He wasn't doing the breathing exercises he taught. I was.

"But since you show such great spirit, how about this. How about I invite you into today's seminar absolutely free of charge, as my personal guest?"

I poked him in the chest with my folded-up twenty. "How about you hand over the CDs?"

He looked like he was thinking, *Will anyone come if I scream?* His back was to the hotel, a beige rectangle floating above his left shoulder an acre of blacktop away.

I turned and walked away. When I turned back, he was jogging toward the safety of the lobby, his shit-brown shoulder bag banging against his ass.

I killed time smoking cigarettes in the woods across the highway, then went back. On older cars like he had, the trunk lock is a piece of cake. I grabbed a set of the Business Yoga CDs. There was a binder, and I took that, too.

The binder turned out to contain a manifesto called *The Power of B-Rays*. The *B* stands for Boogie. I read the whole thing in one sitting. Highly advanced shit. It started with the breathing exercises, but went much further. I read it a second time and took notes. I reduced its message to an index card I still have in my wallet. One side says:

> For peace and courage,
> expand chest
> & admit Boogie Rays.
>
> If in doubt, see other side.

The other side says:

> Do Boogie Rays exist?
> Existence and nonexistence are not
> qualities relevant to Boogie Rays.
>
> See other side.

I put the manifesto in an envelope with three hundred dollars and mailed it back to Biz Yoga Guy.

B-Rays were now flooding in with every drag of my cigarette. I was overflowing with good feelings there on top of the hamper in Lito's closet.

There was a sound. A stab of static followed by a voice. "Lito better stay home today. It might not be safe for Mr. Lito."

The voice was coming from inside the room. What would have been panic was a pinprick on the surface of accumulated B-Rays. I stepped out of the closet and looked around the room. It was unchanged.

"You fuck me, I fuck you," said the voice. It was coming from the giraffe in the cinder block.

I went back to the closet to think that over. It didn't do any good. I still had no idea what'd just happened. And still didn't twenty minutes later when there was a different sound. A key turning in the lock.

It sounded like someone trying to be quiet. The door squeaked open in a slow, sneaky way, then whoever it was moved fast. I couldn't see him as he shot Lito. Through the crack of the door, I saw Lito's corpse jump four times. Then he was gone.

I went after him. But not right after. I didn't want that idiot to shoot me. Five seconds after, snatching the giraffe from the cinder block on the way out the door. In the hallway the door to the stairs was pulling itself closed. I threw myself through it and down six flights of stairs, hitting the landing with my good foot each time and crashing against the wall.

I spilled onto the sidewalk and looked left. A young couple and a skinny teenager. I looked right. Four people, all walking by themselves, including a guy in a black hooded sweatshirt. I took a breath and yelled "Hey!" as loud as I could while looking both ways. Everyone turned their heads except the guy in the sweatshirt. That guy started trotting.

I followed in my gimpy, skipping version of running. He looked back and began to sprint. His feet pointed out like a duck's. I started pushing off a little harder with my bad foot, seeing stars with every step. He turned at the corner. I rounded just in time to see him go into a hotel next to the hospital.

He wasn't in the lobby. There were three ways he could have gone: the elevator, the stairs, or the restaurant off the lobby. A woman was standing protectively in front of her child.

"Sorry, did you happen to see which way my friend—"

Gripping her kid with one hand, she pointed with the other at the restaurant.

I gimp-sped around the hostess stand and skipped like a little ballerina around chairs pulled out to make way for the vacuum. It was the dead hour between lunch and dinner. I pushed through swinging doors to the kitchen.

A dishwater and broth smell. And a door in the back closing. Two faces under white caps turned from the door to me and then back to the door as I slammed through it and into the alley and finally got a good look at him. The back of him anyway. He was dressed all in black like a little kid's idea of a bad guy. He was close but out of reach, separating at twenty-five miles per hour on the back of a garbage truck.

I counted eight witnesses. The six people who'd turned to look when I yelled, lobby mom, and the pair in the kitchen. The giraffe crackled and said, "Haha! Fuck you!"

A failure of charm

From camp to camp, through the foul womb of night
The hum of either army stilly sounds

I WAS BACK IN the coffee shop, making myself familiar to the toddler men of TechCo and tapping in time to a poem on a dead laptop.

I was making no progress memorizing it, too pissed at Lito for getting himself killed. Twice! It's not like these people were master assassins.

I knew a kid like Lito in seventh grade. Robert. A born victim. Some kids thought it was funny to harass him and call him a chink. One day I saw them surrounding Robert, chattering like monkeys and whapping his head.

"Hey Robert, do some kung fu."

"Hey Robert, where are my dumplings?"

They were standing, he was sitting. The sight of his head hanging between his knees and swaying from side to side with their blows became too much.

I came up behind the leader and smashed his head with a rock. A big rock. He dropped to the ground and yelled like he'd never been hit before. He probably hadn't.

"Fuck! Fuck!"

"Shut up for a second," I said. "I need to explain something to you."

"Fuck! Jesus! Fuck!" He was bleeding from his ear.

"Seriously, shut up. You're going to miss this. Look at Robert. Does he look like a chink to you? Do you even know what a chink is? No, you don't, because you're dumb as this rock."

"Get him," said one of the other boys, finally recovering himself.

I smashed him in the head, too, and he joined his buddy on the ground.

"No, don't get me, I'm not done explaining this to you. This is important. Chink is a word for Chinese people. Robert is Filipino. Now look at me. My mom is Japanese. So I'm not a chink either. But close enough for you. See my eyes? See this part? It's called an epicanthic fold, like Chinese people have, and Koreans."

I wasn't sure if they were getting all this, but I continued. "You could call me a chink and you'd be in the right ballpark. Now look at Robert. No eye fold."

Even the two boys on the ground were quiet. I think they were actually listening.

"Also, they don't do kung fu in the Philippines. Robert, what do they do in the Philippines?"

Robert looked more freaked out than his tormentors. "I don't know."

"He doesn't know. Maybe hit people in the head with rocks. It doesn't matter. The thing for you fucking idiots to remember is that Robert is not a chink."

The bell rang for us to come in from lunch. No one moved.

"Robert, don't you have a big brother or something?"

He shook his head.

"That's too bad. But someone else might. So you should stick to sucking each other off. Some of us chinks are less friendly than others."

They all knew about my brother. He was a murderer. That was how I could pull the shit I did. He'd killed a kid in a fight the year before. Got away with it even though everyone knew. He was proud of it. He'd throw his arm around me and say, "Anyone bugging you, buddy? Anyone who needs to be killed?"

He did love me in his way.

I saw a picture of the kid he killed when a cop came around to scare us into talking. The kid's face was intact. "The skull is like a helmet," the cop said, "protecting the insides of your head, which are soft. Your brother broke this boy's helmet." He lightly touched the back of my head. "Kicked his soft stuff all over the ground."

Robert followed me as we went back in from lunch that day.

"Hey, Pope."

"Don't just sit there when people fuck with you, OK? And don't talk to me. I don't know you."

The hum of either army stilly sounds . . .

"No, seriously, what are you doing?" Auburn-dye-job girl was already sitting down.

"Are you a fucking ninja?"

"Yes, I'm a fucking ninja. What are you doing?"

"I thought we covered this."

"I should call security."

"Why do you care?"

"Because you're the only interesting thing I've seen all week."

"Maybe we should leave things as they are then. I might disappoint you once you got to know me."

"I doubt that." That up-and-down look of hers again. "You don't belong here, do you?"

"Why do you say that?"

"Your shirt is ironed, for starters."

I'd been trying to blend in better, but wasn't about to stop ironing my shirt. The collar doesn't lie right otherwise.

"So give it up. Just tell me."

I could see two of me in her glasses. "I'm killing time until I can get in to talk to a guy."

"In where?"

"The building. TechCo. Where you work."

"Why would I work there?"

"How else did you pay for those cute shoes?"

"Maybe I'm blackmailing my married lover."

"He must not be that rich if you still have to wear that TechCo key card."

"OK, now I'm losing interest." For the second time, she got up and left. I didn't follow her this time. I was pretty sure she wasn't losing interest.

I limped to the downtown library to check for news about Lito. There wasn't much. Nothing about him getting shot after he was already dead. Nothing about family, no indication of who'd water his spider plant.

"A flower delivery man is being sought as a person of interest." It didn't say that anywhere.

I also got the low-down on "Tele-fection Critters," which is what the tag on the Giraffe said. The Critters are special plush toys that can receive phone calls. Call and leave a message for your little one when you can't be there. Sorry about the divorce. Daddy loves you.

"It's me again. Detective Boise."

The dusty phone booth in the lobby of the library still worked. I was talking to the university operator.

"We talked a minute ago. About Sandy Sandbag. You said you can't give out her number, and then we got disconnected."

"Sir—"

"I was just wondering if maybe she's in class now and if maybe you could call her on the PA?"

"We don't have a PA."

I asked if she was sure and she hung up on me again. Back at the library computer, I looked up Sandbag's class schedule for the current semester. She was getting out of a Shakespeare lecture in forty-five minutes. I paid the library a quarter to print out a campus map and caught the number forty-eight bus to Plankton U.

The campus put up a good front of pillars and land-scaping, but inside it was bad lighting and battered chairs. I fell into step next to Sandbag in the hallway of Mean Hall. I had to speed—she walked like there was a rocket in her ass. She hardly glanced at me.

"If you need a syllabus, the TAs have them."

"No. I'm Frank Boise, I've been hired by the Cranberries to look into Ed's death."

She stopped. "Oh. Shit. OK. We can talk in my office."

Sandbag eyed me across a big metal desk. In a watercolor on the wall behind her a blobby blue fish was doing something to another blobby blue fish. I sat in a wooden chair opposite and asked how Ed Cranberry's career had been going.

"It was stalled. He was frustrated and bored."

"But you liked him."

"I wouldn't say that. I felt bad for him."

"But he seemed to be doing OK. Nice house."

"I think he made some investments early in his career. And he was in some kind of group fund thing. He tried to bring some of the other faculty in on it."

I wrote *Group fund thing*. "But you weren't interested."

"There were meetings. I don't do anything if there are meetings."

"Was he happy at home?"

"Who's happy at home?"

"I wouldn't know. Did he have a mistress?"

"That word is problematic for a number of reasons."

"So yes?"

"Everyone knew about that."

"What was her name?"

"I don't know if I can tell you that."

"You can't tell me something everyone knows?"

"That's her story, not mine."

"This is strictly for the family. I'm not going to the police. Mayfern hired me to get certain answers the police don't care about. It would really help her healing process."

"Mayfern always looks so lost."

"You should see her now. You can help her out of a dark hole here."

She consulted a jade plant in the window. "Junko Horiuchi. A former student. I don't know anything else."

I wrote the name down, under *Group fund thing*. She told me more stuff. Nothing useful.

I convinced a librarian that I was a student and looked up Junko Horiuchi's address on a computer at the university library in a student directory anyone on the network could see. I exited the library in Junko's direction.

Her apartment building was five blocks from campus, on a street of other apartment buildings. It had rusty railings and bottles in the windows.

The half-hearted rain became full-hearted. She didn't answer the door. I found inadequate shelter under a deformed elm in a square of chemically processed red gravel. I squatted there for a smoke and to soak in the afternoon's B-Rays.

Students shuffled by. Some looked blank and some looked worried. None looked in my direction. Time passed like a candy ribbon through my brain. A woman pulled up on a scooter, straight black hair hanging out the back of her helmet. Her matching skirt and jacket could have been a stewardess uniform.

"Hi Junko." I showed her my palms. She froze in the middle of taking off her helmet.

"What is it?"

I said what I hoped was Japanese for, "Sorry to bother you, but can we talk for a second?" I waited for her to smile at my pronunciation like my aunts in Japan. She didn't. They think I'm cute over there. Junko didn't think I was cute. She saw my blood-filled eye and measured the distance between us.

"I need to tell you something about Ed Cranberry."

Everyone wants to know about their ex. Her shoulders relaxed a little. "What about him?"

"I know he was an asshole. I'm on your side. Sorry, I should introduce myself. I'm Frank Boise."

"You are not Frank Boise," she said, tensing up again. "Frank Boise is a black man." A couple across the street had stopped and were looking at us, the guy with his cell phone out.

"I know! Isn't that funny? I get that all the time, 'Hey, you're not black!' Don't I know it! But no, what I said was I'm *from* Frank. I'm his representative. Peter Johnson. *Hajimemashite.*"

I stuck out a hand. She stared at it.

"Is there somewhere we can talk?"

"It is my apartment," she said, gesturing at the building I'd been squatting in front of, her doubts about me apparently gone.

Her place was manically tidy but had that dusty smell you can't get rid of in old buildings. I took the seat she offered in her nook.

"So remind me how you know Frank."

"From the group." She sat like a contestant in a posture contest at a POW camp.

"You look happy."

"Excuse me?"

"There."

I pointed to a photo on the wall behind her of Junko and a man. The man was baby faced and had a little paunch. They were on a bridge somewhere, pine trees in the background, grinning like only people who've recently started fucking each other can. The frame had two cartoon bears on it and the words *A Friend Indeed Is a Joy Forever.*

"It is my personal item."

"Of course. So, the group. How long were you in it?"

"I was not in it."

"But didn't you meet Frank there?"

"You're his friend. You should know how I met him."

"His representative. I think he told me, but can you remind me?"

"It was about the divorce of Ed. I met Frank to tell him about Ed . . . and I. But my mind is different now."

"Could you expand on that a bit?"

"I do not understand."

"Me either. Let's start over. The group."

"You are with Frank. So you know."

"*Onegaishimasu.* Tell me your side of it."

"Frank is a good man."

"Oh, the best!"

"He will know what to do. I do not want to talk about it."

I faced the window and scanned the sky with my lungs for fresh B-Rays, but they'd scattered to the far corners of Hello Bay. "So what do you want to talk about?"

"You said there was something to tell. About Ed."

"Right. Of course. So you heard he died."

"Yes." She didn't look too broken up about it.

"Who do you think did it?"

"You said you were going to tell me something." Her hands hadn't moved from her lap since we sat down.

"If you're afraid of anyone, we can help you with that. Me and Frank."

"I am not afraid. They should be afraid of me."

"And why is that?"

"My mind is clean. I have Pete now."

"Believe me, I get it. I'm a big proponent of moving on myself. How about I tell you the thing about Ed and in return you tell me one thing about the group?"

"How do I know you will really tell me?"

"I'll count to three. On three we'll both say our things." She thought about that and nodded.

"Ready? One . . . two . . ."

On three, she said, "They have a place on the island," and I said, "He was an asshole."

She put her hands on the table and half lifted herself out of her chair. "I knew he was asshole. You did not tell me anything."

"Sorry about that. That was just practice. Let's go again. I tell you one thing, you tell me one thing. Ready?"

She glowered, but nodded. On the count of three, she said, "They are friends with drug dealers," and I said, "His farts were stinky."

She stood up. "You are . . ." she said, groping for the words, "fucking with me. I will call the police."

"I'm sorry. Really. I'm not fucking with you."

She was walking to a closet. "No one will fuck with me anymore."

"No, they won't. That's why I'm here."

She was taking something out of a shoebox and pulling tissue off.

"We want to help you with—hey! Whoa! None of that now!"

She was pointing a gun at me. "I kill you now."

"Later. You should definitely kill me, I deserve it, but later. You kill me now, your neighbors will hear. You'll go to prison. Your parents will never see you again."

"My parents are dead."

"What about calling the police? Let's go back to that. They've been looking for me. You'll probably get a big reward."

"Get on your knees."

"Not a problem, I'll just go ahead and do that now. But let's keep chatting, OK? I am listening so well right now, I can't even tell you."

She moved toward me. The look in her eye was not promising. I looked around. The picture with the guy.

"Junko, you kill me, you won't see your boyfriend again. Ever. What's his name? Pete? No more Pete."

Whether that got through to her or not, she changed her mind about killing me as quickly as she'd made it up. "It is toy gun. You must leave now."

"An excellent idea. Excellent. Well, thank you. This has been a real pleasure. I'll just show myself out." I paused with my hand on the doorknob and turned back to her.

"Can I just ask one last thing though? When you said the group had a place on the island, did you mean Endorphin Island?"

Junko's eye twitched.

"Yeah, OK, you're right. Let's call this one good. *Shitsurei shimasu!*"

Outside I lit a cigarette and felt for urine stains. I should have recognized that the gun was fake. I'd used a fake gun myself once. It was during a job I did when I was with the Riders. It happened because of a bet. I said we should rent an apartment near a bank and blend in with the neighborhood. We'd hit the bank and escape by stepping into the apartment.

They pointed out supposed flaws in my plan. So we settled on terms: we'd split rent for three months and if I successfully robbed the bank, we'd split the money. If I was caught, they weren't involved. Of course they agreed. I was taking the initiative as usual. The only risk for them was losing cash from the group fund they were squandering anyway.

I found a place with a back door fifty steps from a branch bank. Two months and three days after moving in, I entered the bank in a black coat, gloves, and a mask made out of a T-shirt. I chose a time when, based on my observations from a bar across the street, they were least likely to have customers. There was no security guard. I stuck a gun in the teller's face and said, "Put eight thousand dollars in this bag and you get to live."

A customer came in.

"Come in!" I told her. "It's going to be OK. Lie down on the floor next to those other people, and you get to live."

I didn't count the money. It looked like a lot.

"OK, last thing, everyone!" I said. "Keep your heads down and count to sixty out loud. Don't cheat! I'll be able to hear if you do. Sixty seconds and this is over."

I didn't need the full minute. By the time they got to forty-five, my disguise was in a dumpster, the cash was sealed inside the back of my TV, and I was opening a beer in my living room. I lay on the floor and watched police lights crawl the ceiling.

Even though my plan worked, it put me off armed robbery. I didn't like the expressions of the people in the bank. They didn't know the gun was a hobby shop fake. One of them told the news she'd been thinking about her son the whole time.

I split everything with the other Riders as promised, but they got it in their heads I was holding back on them. That was the start of the trouble.

Back home, I fried a couple of eggs, smoked some Yick Fung Overlook weed, and opened my map of Plankton on the table.

I wrote down a list of all my new friends on index cards and pinned them to the wall above the map:

Edward Cranberry, 53
    Associate Professor of English
    Member of the group
    Dead

Mayfern Cranberry, 48
    Ex-wife of deceased
    Member of arts boards
    Taker of pills

A failure of charm

Helen Cranberry, 26
    Daughter of deceased
    Waitress at East Sea Sushi

Hector Cranberry, infant
    Grandson of deceased
    No occupation

Junko Horiuchi, about 23
    Ex-girlfriend of deceased
    Irritable person
    Victim & former member of group

Paul Dowell
    TechCo
    Possible group leader

Frank Boise
    Friend of deceased
    My enemy

I took out the slip of paper from the kid in front of unit sixteen that said *Rick Fernmancer* and tacked that at the bottom of the column.

I started a second column of cards for corpse number two.

Lester "Lito" Arroyo, about 45
    Coworker of Helen's at East Sea Sushi
    Gardener for Mayfern, Shady Lane Landscaping
    Dead

Large man, name unknown, about 50
    Coworker of the deceased
    Gardener with Shady Lane Landscaping

Medium-size man, age and name unknown
    Shot Lito when he was already dead
    Wears all black
    A little chubby

Unknown person
    Killer of Lito

George
    A giraffe

I'd decided to call the giraffe George.

Face-to-face with a nasty mouthful

Fire answers fire, and through their paly flames
Each battle sees the other's umber'd face

WHAT'S A PALY flame? I was back to memorizing poetry while a tide of diaper-shaped shorts surged around me and out again and rectangular clouds advanced in columns across the sky outside. The place was empty so I saw her come in this time.

"OK, Jesus. I can't watch anymore. You're an idiot. You want in? Follow me."

She charged out. I took the poem from the screen of my laptop, folded it in half, put it in my back pocket, stood up, closed the laptop, put it under my arm, and walked out of the coffee shop.

My sexy languor somehow didn't slow her. I got outside in time to see her hips swinging at top speed through the lobby doors of TechCo, and had to gimp-skip to catch up.

"Pretty confident I'd follow you, weren't you?"

"So much for the myth of the Asian cock," she said, gripping it like an umbrella handle.

That's not actually the next thing she said. But it's the part my mind slides to when I remember Brenda.

What she actually said was, "Like you've got anything better to do. We're going to be at the door in a second and I'm going to let you in." She made a beep sound in her nose. "Can you do that?"

I tried.

"Never mind. When I hold the door open for you, just pretend you're swiping a card. Don't look back."

She swiped her badge and the door beeped. I swiped an invisible badge and she beeped.

"That was amazing. You sound just like it."

"What's your name?"

"Pope Smith."

She turned around, her eyes flashing. "Is that supposed to be funny? I'm doing you a favor. Don't bullshit me."

"OK, sorry. Frank. Frank Boise."

"I'm Brenda. What else should I know about you?"

"I'm a Virgo. My favorite color is green. I wrestled in high school. For about three weeks. I didn't like how the coach kept asking about my BMs."

"OK, that's probably enough for now. Your timing is good. Everyone's at the all-hands."

We came to a bank of elevators.

"Where are we going?"

"You tell me. You wanted in. You're in."

"A guy named Paul Dowell."

We got in the next elevator and she punched 11.

"I really do appreciate this. I know you could get fired."

"Oh, I don't work here. I was laid off by our out-of-state overlords. Only they never bothered to tell anyone here."

"So what are you . . .?"

"I'm here for the copy toner. To cover what they owe me."

"Why are you telling me this?"

"Who are you going to tell? You don't exactly look like you have a lot of friends."

I could've listed the friends tacked on my wall, but decided to let her point stand. "Most people steal *before* they get fired."

"I wasn't fired. I was laid off. And I'm not stealing, I'm collecting on a debt."

"How do you fence copy toner?"

"I've got a guy."

"So you come here every day, pretend to work, and steal office supplies."

"A girl needs an occupation. Especially if she doesn't have a job."

"But wait, don't they notice there's no toner?"

"I intercept it before it gets inventoried on the first of the month."

"That doesn't make—"

"Shut up about that now. We're here."

We walked down a hallway of offices with sliding-glass doors in wooden frames, the usual clutter of plants and kids' drawings. We made a couple turns. More offices, a kitchen area.

"Aren't you supposed to be at the meeting, too?"

"Nah, I'm a temp. Was a temp. The meeting is only for full-timers. But like I just said, shut up about that now." She stopped. "This is his office."

She slid the door open. "We can wait inside if you wanna talk to him."

"Is that a good idea?"

"It's part of the deal here to act super casual. They drop in on each other all the time. They call them 'pop-ins.'"

"Do you mind if I look around a little bit?"

"Or sometimes they call them 'drive-bys.' Why would I mind? Guy's a prick. Let me keep an eye out though." She glanced at a dollar store–looking digital watch. "The meeting is gonna be out in about five."

There was a model of the Parthenon on a little shelf above Paul Dowell's desk, and some little horses next to it, not to scale. He had a little filing cabinet, with a cushion on top, so someone could sit on it and talk to him. Someone whose life might include sitting on a filing cabinet in a sunless room and talking to Paul Dowell. I opened one of the drawers. Papers.

"What are you looking for?"

"Not sure yet." I pocketed some bills and other mail.

"Hey, who said you could take stuff?"

"Oh, you can and I can't?" There was an envelope of photos. I pocketed those, too.

"Jesus, take the whole place, why don't you? OK, shit, sit down. Here he comes." She sat down on Paul Dowell's chair. I sat on the padded filing cabinet and opened my laptop.

Paul Dowell, TechCo, slid open the door and stepped in. His mama's boy face split open on a fortune in orthodontics.

"Well! It's a party!"

"Sure is. Hope we didn't get too wild in here for you." Brenda was suddenly a lot more animated. Smiling. Brushing her hair from her face. "It looks like the meeting was a success. I sense your morale is definitely lifted. You're glowing."

"Oh indeed! Quite fired up am I! The Power-Pointage was truly extraordinary." His nose had a mind of its own, pointing around the room petulantly. I smiled, a silent little doggy in the corner.

"Paul, I'd like you to meet Frank, my new intern."

"*Your* intern?"

"Well, ours, but he'll be shadowing me his first few weeks."

I smiled again. Quiet, humble.

"I think I've seen you in the coffee shop."

"I've been making it my unofficial office while they get me settled in."

"Well, welcome aboard, Frank. I have to warn you we're all crazy here. Brenda is the worst of all!"

"Be nice, Paul. You're going to scare him."

"So what're you going to be working on, Frank?" Another flash of orthodontics.

Brenda answered for me. "The v-next refresh that Priyanka is driving."

"I'm hoping to get a better handle on the paly flames," I volunteered.

She murdered me with her eyes and turned back to Paul. "We'll let you go. You should get some work done while you're still jazzed up from that all-hands."

"Yes, after that, who knows! I could do some serious damage!"

We agreed it was nice to meet each other, then Brenda and I were gone.

"You got any plans for the rest of the afternoon?"

"I sure as fuck can't come back here now."

A meeting of
the minds

I OPENED THE DOOR to my apartment. My living room chair was on top of the coffee table in the middle of the room.

"I like what you've done with the place."

"I like to take in the view while I dine. Like a sea captain."

"Is that what a sea captain does?"

"Do you want some green tea or something?"

"Greeen teeeeea. Greeny weeny teeny. Sure."

When I came back with it she was doing something with a mirror and lipstick. I put the tea down on the floor. "May I kiss you?" I said.

"We can try it and see how it goes."

She kissed in low gear. We moved to the sofa and kissed some more. Her skirt hiked up her thighs. I pushed her down and slid between her legs and got her hose and panties down.

"I didn't shower this morning," she said.

"Good." I licked her pussy slowly from the bottom to the top, lightly, then intrusively. I gripped her clit with my lips and sucked. She reached down to pull her skin up to more fully expose it. I slid two fingers in and she started pumping her hips on my hand.

"Keep doing that for a while." She had a hand in my hair.

"Mmmmkmm."

We ended up in my bed, losing the rest of our clothes on the way. "So much for the myth of the Asian cock," she said, gripping it like an umbrella handle.

When we got to the actual fucking, things went more quickly than I'd planned. "And you started out so well," she said.

"You looked like you could use a break."

She propped herself up on one elbow. "Can we move back to the living room, please?"

"Why?"

"Because now we're getting to the part where we feel false intimacy. It makes it confusing later."

"You're the last of the true romantics, eh?"

With the speed of a lizard, she pulled out one of my pubic hairs.

"Ouch! Jesus!"

"Now we're even."

"For what?"

She put her top and skirt and glasses back on. But not her underwear. She got up to pee, then I did. I noticed my hair was perfect. We moved back to the couch and drank room-temperature green tea. "Not to make you feel false intimacy or anything, but my name really is Pope."

She didn't look surprised. "Last name?"

"Smith."

"Did your parents hate you, Pope Smith?"

"My dad was a Christian in some complicated way. He said the institution of the pope was a historical accident and so was I. He eventually started fucking the women in his New Directions spirituality group."

"And this explains why you're like this or something?"

"Something. Hey, did you fix my hair when I was going down on you?"

"I might have. It was bothering me."

"Weren't you supposed to be lost in the throes of ecstasy?"

"What are those?" She'd spotted the cards pinned to my wall.

"A project I'm working on."

"Related to Paul Dowell?"

"No. Completely unrelated."

"Is that why there's a card that says 'Paul Dowell'?"

"I thought my handwriting was too messy to read."

"What are you talking about? You write like a girl."

"Thanks."

"So what's the project? Are you stealing from all these people?"

"Is that all you think about?"

"'Irritable person'—what does that mean?"

I tried to think of a reason not to tell her, and couldn't. So I did. I got as far as discovering Ed Cranberry's foot at Yick Fung Overlook. "So Boise sent me there as some kind of setup, but what was supposed to happen? Was I supposed to be ID'd by the red hat and arrested for murder? What kind of plan is that?"

"Angry is a good look for you." Her eyes were shining behind her thick lenses. "Your hair needs fixing again though."

Bent over my couch getting fucked with her skirt still on was a good look for her. Afterward, I went down on her until she came.

"As I was saying," I continued, wiping my mouth, "the plan was apparently to kill the guy, dump the body at a public park, and have a random guy in a red cowboy hat on hand just in case?"

"I'm not sure I believe any of this."

"It must be a burden to be such a suspicious person."

"It would help if you occasionally said something that wasn't totally absurd."

"Bitch!"

I didn't say that. George did.

"That was George."

"Of course it was."

"Do you want a cocktail? I make a pretty good gimlet."

"I'll have a glass of white wine, please." She didn't mind having it in a jelly jar. I made a gimlet for myself.

When we were settled back in bed with our drinks, she said, "So why are you here? In Plankton."

"Well, there was a woman. And trouble with some friends . . ."

"What was her name?"

"Lisa."

"We'll come back to Lisa. What friends? What trouble?"

I told her about the Riders. The bank job and the money they wanted from me. And the bus that ran over my foot.

"So you actually are a criminal."

"That's an uncharitable interpretation. Especially from an office-supply stealer."

"Right, because that's totally the same thing as robbing a fucking bank."

"It was just an experiment."

"Shut the fuck up. You robbed a bank. You're a bank robber."

"Don't you want to know about George?"

"In a minute. The woman. Lisa."

"I don't like to dwell."

"And Lisa was totally unrelated to the other thing, the trouble with your fellow robbers?"

"Totally."

"Uh-huh. OK, now that you've had time to come up with another pack of lies, who's George?"

I told her about George and how I got him. She was mostly quiet, occasionally asking questions like, "You carried a flower arrangement two miles?" and "Your reaction to finding a dead body was to smoke cigarettes in the closet for three hours?" When I finished, I asked if she believed me now.

"I don't know. Does it matter? It was a good story. I listened to the end anyway."

"Do you get high?"

"No, I don't 'get high.' What are you, twelve years old? I'll take another glass of wine though."

I made myself a second gimlet and brought the wine bottle for her.

She pointed it at me. "But even if it's all true, and there's some kind of stupid conspiracy against you—"

"I never said 'conspiracy.'"

"—it didn't work. You weren't arrested or blamed for anything, so who cares? Why not forget it and move on?"

"I'm sick of people treating me like I'm the ass-hole when they're the asshole."

"That's stupid, but go on."

"Lito. I found him and he doesn't have anyone else. He's my corpse now."

"So you got your feelings hurt, and that somehow became . . . a crusade for a dead landscaper?"

"It's also a matter of standards. The way people go about their business here is a disgrace. Think about it. The way Ed Cranberry was killed and dumped in a public place. The way Lito was shot by two idiots in a row. And the giraffe. And the cowboy hat. The criminals here are a clown car. And the police are too shitty at their jobs to enforce any standards."

"Among the criminals?"

"Yes, among the criminals!"

"When you put it like that, yeah, it sounds perfectly reasonable."

We both drank. "Do you think you could help me scope out Paul Dowell a little more?"

"That's the worst way anyone's ever asked me out. Try again."

"May I . . . buy you a glass of wine?"

She looked at the wine in her hand.

"A different glass of wine. With dinner."

"Keep trying."

"May I have the pleasure of your company at dinner? A dinner at which you'll drink a glass of wine if you'd like?"

"Are you paying, or will this be dine-and-dash?"

"Please! I'll even wear a tie."

"Don't do that. Where are we going?"

"I know a great sushi place where they give you little hot towels to wipe your ass."

"You're lucky I'm so bored right now. Or your chances wouldn't be nearly as good."

"My chances?" I surveyed our naked bodies.

"For whatever else it is you think you want from me. Pick me up at five."

"Sure. Do you mind being picked up by bus?"

She gave me her up-and-down look. "Have my fare ready. I hate people who fumble at the box." She wrote *1 Island Way* on my Rick Fernmancer card. "It's by What Lake."

Flee and fuck

T HERE WAS NO Island Way by What Lake. At least not according to the twenty people I asked. I looked for a phone. No one would let me use theirs. I tried a more aggressive approach with the kid behind the counter at Licky Luke's Ice Cream Parlor. Probably overshot the mark, judging by how he flinched when I took the phone from his hand. But I did get Brenda on the line.

"Hey. Where are you?"

"At home. Waiting for you."

"Which is where? No one's heard of Island Way."

"Oh, that's more of a private name. What I call it."

"Feel free to elaborate."

"Well, where would you expect something called Island Way to be?"

"This isn't the funnest game I've ever played."

"I'm on the island."

"The island."

"The one in the middle of the lake. Go to the boat rental place. You should hurry. They close at five."

"If I put the phone down now and sprint the whole way, I might make it. But as you know, I'm a cripple."

"Navigate to a little cove on the west side of the island. Follow the path behind the No Trespassing sign."

I made it to the rental place. Barely. It was a nice evening and there'd been a run on canoes. All they had left were paddleboats shaped like swans. The surface of the lake was orange from the sky. I rounded the island and found the cove and the sign. Securing my swan in the mud, I followed the path. The lake vanished behind a curtain of forest. The cottage at the end of the path looked old but solid. Clean windows and lights on inside. Brenda opened the door before I knocked.

"How the hell is there a house here and how did you get it?"

"You want to come in?"

"I'd love to, but our reservations are in 30 minutes and we're a swan and two buses away."

She marched ahead of me in heels, holding my arm when we crossed mud. The swan went a lot faster with two pedaling.

"So what's the story with that place?"

"It was built by some eccentric decades ago. Grandfathered in."

"And you own it?"

"Some guy does. We have an arrangement."

"Can I ask what kind of—"

"Nope. None of your business."

"Wait, so how do you get back and forth?"

"Oh, I have my own swan. I stash it in the pussy willows on the island and cattails on the shore."

We got a seat in the back of the bus. As it crested King's Crown, she leaned in and kissed me and said into my ear, "Your stories don't add up."

"Not sure what you mean."

"I want you to know that I know."

"That's a lot of knowledge."

East Sea Sushi was packed. While I told the hostess about our reservation, Brenda wandered over to the sushi bar and sat down. I sat next to her.

"We have a table."

"We have to sit here. It's the only way to keep an eye on them." She inclined her head at the two sushi chefs. One of them looked up.

"You are aware that we're not currently in a soundproof booth, right?"

She turned around in her seat to talk to a passing server. "We need sake. A big hot one and two cups, please." She turned back to me. "It's a money thing, not a cult thing. The murder, I mean."

"Maybe we should grab that table?"

"Don't be ridick. Those guys aren't listening."

They clearly were. "OK then. Shoot. Money, murder, cult. Be sure to enunciate the names of everyone you mention."

"The way you kept saying 'The Group' made it sound like it was some kind of cult. Paul isn't sexy enough to run a cult. But the investment club Professor Sandbag mentioned, the one Ed Cranberry was in. Paul started something like that. Tried to get people at work to come listen to him present financial self-improvement tips over wine and cheese. No one went. We thought it was a joke. I bet it was the same group Ed was in."

"What about the place on Endorphin Island Junko told me about?"

"How should I know? I can't solve the whole thing for you. God!" She slammed a few cups of sake in rapid succession. "But I will tell you one more thing—you should forget about finding out why Boise sent you to Yick Fung."

"Why?"

She drained another cup. "Why do they serve this stuff in thimbles? Who cares, is why. It's a side issue. You have to look into what ties all these people together. The Group. That's the only decent lead you have." Brenda was waving the empty sake bottle at a red-haired busboy across the room.

One of the sushi chefs—the shorter, squatter one—sliced a *kappa maki* into six pieces and deployed them in an arrangement with a gleaming pile of sashimi and pretended not to listen. Coming here probably wasn't the best call.

"Shouldn't we order some food? You promised me dinner."

"Sure. Excuse me!"

The sushi guy looked up like he'd just noticed us. I ordered spicy tuna rolls and vegetable tempura. There was a picture in a black frame behind the sushi bar, with flowers around it. It wasn't a picture of Lito.

"Who's the dead guy?" I asked. We couldn't possibly be any more conspicuous anyway.

"The owner's father."

"How about your coworker? Where's his picture?"

His face went from confused to disturbed. "Excuse me?"

"Didn't you recently lose one of your fellow sushi chefs?"

"We've already talked to the cops."

"You seem to be taking it very well. Let me ask you something else." He gripped his knife and didn't look at the printer spitting an order at him. "Is Tatsu working today?"

"He'll probably pop in any second," said someone behind me.

Helen Cranberry. She looked less friendly each time I saw her. "I didn't see you here."

"Oh look, it's Frank Boise. I'm not working the sushi bar tonight, Frank Boise. I've got a floor section, Frank Boise." She nodded at the room of Caucasians politely waiting for *maguro*. "So, Frank Boise, have you found my dad's killer yet?"

"You'll be the first to know."

Brenda held up the empty sake bottle. "As long as you're here, can we have another one of these?"

"Not my section."

Helen marched to a dark hallway in the back of the restaurant. Her silhouette leaned into another silhouette. The second silhouette emerged into the light. A tall guy with a scar on his neck, his glare eclipsed by a smile upon eye contact.

"Sorry your ST rolls are taking so long! Please have a round of sake on me while you wait!"   T h e scar on his neck was faintly pulsing.

"You must be the famous Tatsu." Did he just shorten spicy tuna to "ST"?

His glare flashed before he managed to clap his smile back on.

I grabbed Brenda after he left. "I need to tell you something. Outside. Bring your coat."

In the hallway, Brenda staggered a little. "If you're planning to fuck me in the men's room, forget it. By which I mean, you'll have to get me a LOT drunker than this."

"Thanks for the tip. But no. We gotta vamoose."

"What?"

"I'm pretty sure they called the cops on us."

"Great, I really am dating a fucking criminal."

"Here. Stairs."

"God knows why you think you're worth this much trouble." She took off her heels and we stumble-limped arm in arm down six flights of stairs. Panting on the street, she turned her open mouth to me and I kissed her against a wall, then steered her by her shoulders toward a taxi stand in front of a hotel a couple blocks away. I routed our driver past East Sea Sushi. A police cruiser was blazing outside.

By the time we were home, my throat hurt from laughing and I had a smear of lipstick on my neck. She was out of her top before we were all the way in the door.

Driven sideways

BRENDA SAID NO to coffee. "Tennis date with my sister."

"I guess I forgot to mention I have a French press? We can have it in the living room. Black and bitter as your heart. No intimacy."

"No. Really. I gotta go." She closed the door and George cackled at it. "Knock knock, you're dead!"

I massaged her perfunctory kiss into my jaw and watched her hips three floors below swing around the corner and out of sight. George had a replay button on one of his teats. I listened to the message a dozen more times—*Knock knock, you're dead*—then got out the water bill and other mail I swiped from Paul Dowell's office. It was all addressed to the same place on the What Lake side of Plankton. Except an electricity bill that'd been sent to an address on Endorphin Island: 13 Charity Lane. I decided to go there first so I'd have more to ask him about when I visited Paul Dowell at his home.

I also found Brenda's panties balled up under my bed and thought it would be pretty smooth to return them on my way there. Even if it was the opposite direction. I biked down to the lake and got a regular canoe instead of a swan and pulled it onto the mud like before.

"What?" The voice through the cottage door sounded like a different person.

"Hey, it's Pope."

"So?"

"So you may remember me from a few hours ago? I think I was spanking you at one point?" The door was quiet. "So, yeah. You forgot something. Can I come in for a sec? I won't stay."

She said nothing some more, then said, "It's open." I pushed on the door. It was blocked from inside. Shouldering through, I found a stack of cardboard boxes labeled OfficeSmart Copy Toner.

"What is it?" She was on the couch with the lights out and the curtains drawn, one leg on the floor like she'd dropped it there and couldn't be bothered to pick it up.

"You should have told me you needed help fencing this stuff."

"It's OK."

"You forgot these." Turns out it's not easy to casually twirl panties on your finger. Not enough heft.

"OK."

"So you want to grab sushi again later this week?" Flop sweat was forming on my brow.

"Yeah, no. I don't know."

"There were at least three answers there. I'll take the first one. What's going on with you?"

"Do you need an accounting of my every reaction?"

"When you put it like that . . ."

"Look, I don't need fixing. And I can't fix whatever your problem is right now."

"OK, sorry to bother you."

She sat up. "Did you think you got a receipt when you stuck your dick in me?"

I didn't follow that, but the floor didn't seem to be open for questions.

I paddled back in defeat. Outside the boat place, I laid eyes on a man in camouflage pants and a knit cap with flames on it. At that exact moment, a surge of

B-Rays broke over my face like a stinging liquid and a vision of the boy from Resentment Court appeared to me. I looked into the man's eyes and all the way through him. I said, "Rick Fernmancer?"

His head snapped at his name. "Yes?"

I delivered a five-dollar punch to his nose. He held it and yelled. I scampered off to find my bike before a crowd formed.

The outside of a Hello Bay ferry at night looks like a glowing palace. The inside of a Hello Bay ferry during the day looks like a cafeteria. I sat in a booth and watched Plankton shrink.

I didn't use to be violent. It changes how you look at people. It did me anyway. If it came to it, would I take them or would they take me? I began to review potential hand-to-hand strategies against randos in the grocery store. Clavicle clawing followed by dick kicking? Elbow-twisting, car-key-eyeball-stabbing combo? I got my moves from a women's self-defense class. They couldn't think of a reason to keep me out. The basic strategy is to attack joints, soft tissue, and small bones. I ended up playing the attacker in a padded suit. I was kneed, elbowed, and gouged by a succession of shouting women. I always had to rush home to jerk off after class.

The speakers in the ferry yelled at everyone to get back to their cars. The impact of the rubber buffers of the Endorphin Island ferry dock shivered through the hull. I walked off with my bicycle. The stores around the terminal sold fudge and keychains with dolphins on them. A few blocks in, there was a place called the Solstice Cafe that looked like it catered to locals. I got directions to Charity Lane from a gray-haired lady in sandals behind the espresso machine. In my biking gear I looked like any other Plankton dork out for the day. Even with my bloody eye. She said Spine Road ran through the center of the island and that Charity was two turns off Spine, and also did I know Endorphin was technically a rain forest?

The corner of Spine and Charity was choked with ferns and pines. The air was heavier inland. Charity turned from dirt to gravel, and I ditched my bike behind a tree. It was a good quarter-mile walk between driveways. Paul Dowell's driveway was five driveways in. The quiet became more quiet at the end of it. There was no house, just two trailers facing each other across a fire pit. I smashed the door handles of both trailers with a rock from the fire pit and retreated to the top of a tree to have a cigarette and see if anyone had heard me. If anyone did, they didn't come running. A chain saw whined miles away.

I climbed down and went into the first trailer. Futons on the floor and a stack of books. A Tanakh. A Bhagavad Gita. A book about making money by having the right attitude. The second trailer was being used as an office. Some stationery on the desk said *Sky Limits, LLC.* There was also a shoe box of slides. I put it into my pack.

It was downhill all the way back to the ferry. My hands on the handlebars were sticky with pine sap.

I spent the evening with a vodka and juice, holding the slides up to the bathroom light. Paul Dowell and his nose in most of them. One showed a group of people in old-timey costumes, including Ed Cranberry in a monocle and top hat. And someone I didn't expect: Helen Cranberry. She was in a dozen slides, raising a glass of wine, listening intently to something, laughing with her arm around Paul Dowell. All apparently taken on the same occasion, in some kind of banquet room.

Another surprise: Lito standing next to his fellow Shady Lane landscaper. Lito was in a little ruffled shirt and sky-blue jacket. It could have been a costume, but maybe that was really how he dressed up. His coworker towered over him in a black jacket and cuff links that caught the camera's flash.

Lito was actually who I wanted to talk to, but he wasn't available. And I didn't know where his charming coworker was. But Helen could tell me. She would probably be off work in half an hour. I changed into my bike suit, coasted downtown, and climbed the stairs to the roof of the parking garage across from East Sea Sushi.

She was visible in the window across the street. I added three butts to the baby bamboo can while she charged around wiping things. After disappearing into the back, she passed through the sky bridge and materialized on the garage roof, moving briskly toward her '88 Cilantro.

"Hey Helen, it's me!"

I stepped in front of her too quickly. She took her hand from her purse and brought out something that went *chhhh* into my face and made my eyeballs boil out of my skull. I doubled over and hacked until snot was pouring out of my nose. I tried to say *Oh fuck*. It came out *Aw fa*.

Helen seemed to be on the phone. "Yes, white male, twenties or thirties, hard to tell. Ugly. Brown hair, bike pants. You'll find him crying in the corner."

I was breathing in through my mouth and out through my nose trying to get the fumes out of my nasal passages. "I'm . . . not white!"

"He's not white. What are you?"

"Let's . . . no . . . police."

"I don't know what he is. Yes, the top of the parking garage. This is the same guy we called you about last night. Yep, East Sea Sushi. Bring lots of guns."

"Helen . . ."

"He says to tell you he really wants to kill some pigs tonight."

"Helen . . . police . . . I'll tell . . . everything." I hacked some more. "Paul . . . your dad . . . Endorphin . . ."

I wasn't going to get any more words out. My eyes were sealed in flame. I was feeling for the wall so I could follow it and find the stairs when I felt Helen grab me by my reflective bike vest and propel me in the opposite direction.

"Get in, fuckface." She put my hand on a car door. She was out of her spot and flooring it before I was fully sitting down. The engine sounded rough.

"One of your belts . . ." I said. ". . . maybe . . . timing belt . . . loose."

"Don't talk now."

If I was talking, people in Plankton generally wanted me to stop. We turned in tight circles until the spiral ramp shit us into the street and down the block, sirens at our back. I'd missed my second chance in two nights to meet the Plankton Police.

My nose was still a mighty river of snot. We drove for a while to the sound of me sniffling and trying to hold my face together. There were no B-Rays to be had, but I used some Biz Yoga to get my breathing under control. By the time Helen turned off the engine, I could open my eyes a little.

"Do you have a tissue?"

She handed me a newspaper. I used it to wipe the snot and tears off my face. It didn't work very well. She laughed. A little, then like she would never stop. "You look so . . . stupid . . . you . . . ink all over your face . . . oh my God . . ." Now she was the one having trouble getting words out.

"That's great. Thanks. I'm sure it's very funny."

Her laughter had started to die down when she was overcome by another explosion. "Hey, look at me, I'm Frank Boise, I have a few questions for you! Oh God . . ." She was heaving now, convulsing against her seat and shaking the whole car. "This is my special card!"

"Look, I'm just going to leave."

"I'm Frank Boise and I'm leaving!" She was screaming and pounding her feet, tears pouring down her cheeks. A film of ink and mucus was drying on my face.

"OK, OK, I get it. I deserve it. But before I go, can I ask you about a picture I saw you in?"

She stopped laughing. "Wait, you're *still* trying to ask me questions? Let's review real quick, shall we?

You tell me you're someone you're not so you can get into my house, right after my dad was fucking murdered. A stranger, a fucking pervert in my house, right next to my son!"

"Now hold on—"

"Then you fucking follow me to work. You come INTO where I work. You go to my MOTHER'S house, where you're ALONE with her. You come BACK to the restaurant with some slut, and talk all kinds of crazy shit about my dad in front of my coworkers. You run out on your bill."

"I did leave a twenty."

"Your fat girlfriend drank three bottles of sake."

"I don't think it's kind or even accurate to call her—"

"And now you come back AGAIN, at night, and wait for me in the fucking parking garage. Sure, how can I be of assistance?"

"You make some good points. Some really good points."

"You should be dead, you know that? Most people who were you would be dead. If I'd had a gun just now when you jumped out at me the city would've given me a medal."

"Your dad liked guns?"

"Oh God, why am I talking to you?"

"Maybe it would help if I were a little more forth-coming about who I am."

"No, it would help if you would stay the fuck away from me and my family. But, yeah, since you're here one last time, who are you?"

"My name is Pope Smith. I'm new in town. Virgo. Favorite color is green. I got into something with Frank Boise and I wanted to find out what."

"So you go around pretending to be him. That makes perfect sense."

"That's how it started, but along the way, there was another killing. Your coworker."

"Lito? What's Lito to you? You his cousin or something?"

"Yes, we're all related."

"But why *pretend* to investigate my dad's murder if all you care about is Lito?"

"He wasn't part of the plan."

"What fucking plan? You know what? Never mind. We're done. Get out."

"Can I just ask you about the picture? The one of you with Paul Dowell? It must mean something since we just ran away from the cops."

She blew her nose.

"Hey, you *do* have tissues!"

"New box. Didn't want to open it. Out." She raised the pepper spray.

I got out and trotted by the car as she reversed into the street. "Just tell me where we are," I asked through the window before it rolled all the way up.

"North Hello. Don't come around anymore. The cops know you now. Everyone does."

"Don't come around where?"

"Anywhere."

Grand entrance wound

THERE WAS A knock. The apartment manager. He looked like he hadn't taken a decent shit in forty years. Wanted to know about the lady with the dog and the conversation we'd had in the courtyard about smoking in the building.

"What can I say? There are a lot of drunks in this place."

"The report was that you were the one who'd been drinking."

"A twilight cocktail. Do you even know what that is?"

"This kind of thing is grounds for eviction. May I ask why your furniture is stacked up like that?"

"I have to keep the floor clear. I sublet it to some tiny men. They use it as a landing strip for their airplane."

"Mr. Smith—"

"A little bomber. I'd show it to you but they're out on their rounds now."

"I need you to understand—"

"They strafe the shit out of the neighborhood cats, let me tell you what." I pointed a tiny invisible machine gun at him. "*Chu-chu-chu-chu-chu-chu.*"

". . . anything that interferes with the safety—"

I continued making machine gun sounds until he left. The giraffe said, "You're dead."

My dad used to say we love people because they die. If they lived forever, they'd lose their value. This from a man who tossed Mom like garbage. "We're the only species that dies, and the only species that loves," he told me when I was ten.

"We're not the only species that dies."

"The only one that knows it though."

He never saw a wake for a crow. I did. One crow standing over the body of another on a park sidewalk. Ignoring people walking by. Didn't even move when some kids started throwing rocks. They stopped when I had a word with their leader and also broke his pinky. I beat a tactical retreat when the kid's dad got involved. Boy was that guy mad.

Anyway, death. Why threaten? Why not do? This was the third message from the man on the other side of George. A man with time on his hands and a need to chat. There had been something going in the background after he finished talking. A muffled conversation. I hit George's nipple to replay the message. I could only make out "your large . . . mushrooms . . ."

I wrote that down on a card and put it on the wall with the other cards. I rearranged them to put Paul Dowell's name in the middle. There were direct lines from Paul Dowell to Helen, Junko, Ed, and Mayfern. I made a card for Brenda and pinned that up, too. Another direct line to Paul.

Since I'd already seen his little cult headquarters on Endorphin Island, it was time to visit the other address I had for him, his home on the What Lake side of Plankton. I struggled over King's Crown on my bike and coasted down the other side. It was the middle of the day, but no kids were out. Kids here didn't skip school and do normal stuff like we did, like breaking windows and getting into people's Tuff Sheds. Some chickadees made a racket in a maple.

The only people in evidence were landscapers working on a yard a few blocks from Paul Dowell's house.
Not Shady Lane.

Paul Dowell lived in a skinny three-story townhome.
I sat on a chair in his yard, still in my helmet and other
bike gear, and had a smoke. I was getting used to spandex. When I wore regular pants I missed the ass pad-
ding. Sitting there for fifteen minutes, I saw a single
car and no pedestrians. Daytime breaking and entering
is a terrible idea, but who was going to see me?

The front door was at a right angle from the
street, in a little canyon formed by two rows of iden-
tical townhomes facing each other across a shared
carport. His lock was a twenty-second task. I got a
beer from Paul Dowell's fridge and sat on his couch.
A poster for a World Cup from a previous decade
sagged in its frame. I turned on the TV and someone
started telling me how to make my own marshmal-
lows. A cat made a tentative appearance from behind
the couch.

I started rifling through his shit. Business books,
frozen food, and some Benzo. His bedroom had piles
of clothes and a dried-out bowl of cereal. An upscale
version of Lito's mess. A second bookcase with a book

on Overcoming LMR, which stood for "Last-Minute Resistance."

I rummaged in his closet. Shitty jeans. A Plankton Half Marathon T-shirt, a grubby ball cap. Back downstairs I turned the thermostat up to eighty-five, opened the windows, and had the rest of my beer.

"Can you wake me in an hour?" The cat had gotten bored with being scared and was stretched out on the windowsill. He blinked slowly. *Danke.* The microwave clock said 3:15. I cupped my balls inside my spandex and fell asleep. I woke up to the cat walking on my throat. The microwave said 4:30. "Hey, I said an hour! It's OK. Close enough."

I made coffee with his French press and put my helmet and tinted goggles back on. I was sitting at his table with a cup, gazing out the window at the ass crack of a woman bending over to pick up her dog's shit, when the downstairs door opened. He'd come up and was dumping his pockets on the kitchen counter when he noticed me.

"Holy fuck!" He started to move toward the stairs. I blocked his way. I'd been nice to everyone I met, and what had it gotten me?

"Why all the Benzo?"

"Help! Call nine-one-one!" He headed for the balcony. Jesus, what a panicker. I grabbed an arm and applied two stiff fingers to his neck.

"Could you please calm down?" He crumpled to the floor and immediately started to get up. I helped him. "I'm just here to install the fan blades."

"What?" He momentarily stopped spazzing.

"I'm your friend's friend. I want to talk. Just talk."

"Who are you?"

"Your friend's . . . Look, I'm nobody. Just sit and talk to me and I'll be gone in ten minutes." He took a seat at the table.

"Why all the Benzo?"

"What? I have a prescription."

"What did you do to Junko?"

The tip of his nose pulsated. "Nothing. What do you mean?"

"Nothing, what do I mean? Junko wanted to kill you. Still does, I think. She wanted to kill me when I asked her about it. What did you do?"

That brought a grimace. "I don't have to talk to you."

"Oh, but you do. Either that, or . . . Oh, let's skip the part where I threaten you. You talk, I leave. Easy for you, easy for me."

"Why are you doing this?"

"Everyone in this town lacks basic conversational skills. And you're part of the problem, Paul Dowell. Stick to the topic. You have a big brother? Ever try to wrestle him? I'm the fourteen-year-old here and you're the eight-year-old. I reset your burr grinder, by the way. With a French press it should be a coarse grind. Do you want a beer? I think you have one left in there. Whoa! You're way too jumpy." He'd thrown his hands in front of his face when I gestured at the fridge.

In the window across the street a woman in a bathrobe was talking to a man in a bathrobe. If they looked over they'd see Paul Dowell talking to a guy in bike gear. I poured the beer into a glass and gave it to him. He hesitated, then picked it up and took a giant swallow.

"Good. Relax. Talk. The Benzo."

He blew air through pursed lips and didn't move.

"You have very healthy color in your cheeks. You look like a German lumberjack in a children's book. You know what I mean?"

He seemed not to. The gears in his brain were grinding. "You're a friend of Chang."

"What?"

"Right? Chang sent you?"

"Sure, yeah. I'm a friend of Chang. Now tell me about Junko." The couple in the bathrobes across the street had disappeared. The cat padded aimlessly by. Paul Dowell looked at the ceiling.

"Junko was a friend of a guy named Ed. I haven't seen her in months."

"Tell me about Ed."

"Can't I just talk to Chang directly if there's some kind of problem?"

Did this dumb motherfucker really think I was sent by someone named Chang? "No. He doesn't want to talk to you anymore. He's doing you a huge favor by sending someone as polite as me."

"What does Chang care about Junko?"

The way he said the name was starting to grate on me. "He goes by Charles now."

"I don't know what Junko told him. We were hanging out and she was drinking and misunderstood what was going on. There was a language barrier."

He recoiled from the pills I dumped on the table. "And it happened in a trailer on Endorphin Island, this thing she didn't understand?" The cat came out to sniff at a few pills that had skittered across the floor.

He said nothing.

"I think I got it. We'll move on now. Tell me about your little group on the island."

"It was a stock-buying club."

"Sounds neat."

"Chang should—"

"Charles."

"Charles should know. It was for people who wanted to pick up investment tips in a casual setting."

"From you?" I looked around his living room-kitchen combo with neighbors in bathrobes peering in.

"Once people understood the value of what we were offering, the momentum was very natural." His nose settled into a self-satisfied lump.

"Impressive stuff. So who started this thing, you or Ed?"

"Me, obviously."

"When did Ed join?"

"Not until it was well under way."

"What did you do to him?"

"Me? Nothing. I assumed that was something on Chang—"

"Charles."

"—on Charles's side of things."

"Charles will be thrilled to hear you just fingered him."

"No, come on! Ch—Charles and I have always worked well together."

"How about Lito?"

"Wasn't Charles also . . .?"

"Also what? Charles was just killing everyone in town?" Paul stared at the surface of the table. "You should get rid of some of this clutter and rethink your furniture. Especially the dead space by the couch. And get some plants. You get great light."

Shadows were rising like a drowning tide over the houses across the street.

"OK, back to Ed. Tell me your story of what happened. Did you do it yourself?"

"I already told you—"

"I know you did. Now tell me something else."

"I don't get what Charles is doing here."

"Not your job to know."

"We were on the same page. We weren't supposed to talk about it. Does he want more money?"

I tipped the World Cup poster off the wall and it shattered on the floor. The cat scampered away. Paul Dowell punched me. It was such a terrible, flailing punch that I hardly bothered to get out of the way. Except it turned out not to be a punch, but a stab.

He'd produced a knife from somewhere when I had my back turned.

I snatched a dining chair and pinned him against the wall. He was defeated even before I got hold of his wrist to get the knife out. I tossed it. The man and woman in bathrobes were back in the window across the street. The man was on the phone.

I made Paul Dowell hand over his cell phone and T-shirt and tied the shirt around my bleeding shoulder. Outside, I surveyed narrowing options. Escaping on foot wasn't a good option, but my bike would be worse. I might make it to the lake and join the army of cyclists going around in circles. But the man in the bathrobe had already ID'd me and a bloody T-shirt bulging at my shoulder wasn't going to help me blend in with the exercise people.

I kept limp-trotting down the street.

Around the corner and two blocks away, I ditched my helmet, cycle goggles, and Paul Dowell's phone in a bush. No sirens yet. They'd probably do a silent approach. Why hadn't I brought a change of clothes? Or even a hat? Plankton was making me soft. Like Paul Dowell's folds of flab after he'd handed over his shirt.

Banh never made plans. When it came time to do something—burglary or getting drinks, it didn't matter—he'd say, "What's the plan?" I could hear him saying it now. Banh was one of the Riders. Maybe I mentioned him already.

A crow jeering from a telephone wire. And another sound. An engine running. Around another corner and there they were. The landscaping crew I'd seen earlier. The truck anyway. It was running and no one was in it. Voices coming from the backyard. I hauled myself into the truck bed and curled up on a pile of mulch under a blue tarp.

"Why you leave it running?"

"Oil has to circulate for a minute."

"It's even not your truck."

"It's about respect. Respect the motor."

Fine particles of mulch stuck to Paul Dowell's T-shirt where I'd bled through. Under the tarp everything was blue. Rain began to patter. It was nice. Like I was already dead.

George gets a charter

I LIMPED TO MY front door. There was an eviction notice taped to it. I limped to the toilet and took a dump and wiped my ass with the notice and limped to the manager's office and jammed it down his mail hole, leaving a little trail of blood drops there and back.

I showered, cleaned my wound, duct-taped a sock to it, and dialed Brenda's number. "I know I'm interrupting your tennis schedule. But I want to ask a favor."

"Why would I do you a favor?"

"Because it could be fun. How about eight?"

"You can't get a boat that late."

"I'll make arrangements."

I found an unattended rowboat at the edge of What Lake and freed it with a bolt cutter. I traveled over the surface of the water and through the trees on the island. Brenda opened her door to find me with a bottle of wine in one hand and a giraffe in the other, shifting from one foot to the other because I'd cut my butthole on a stiff corner of the balled-up eviction notice.

Brenda said, "You do know you made me lose my job, don't you?"

"I'm fine, thanks. Wait, what job? Your fake job?"

"It was still mine. You didn't even say sorry."

"I'm sorry I made you lose your fake job. Honest. And I get that you're occupied with some kind of death spiral of depression. I'm not trying to interfere with that, and I'm also not trying to get in your pants right now. Which look very nice, by the way."

She started to close the door.

"No, no, wait. Thirty seconds. You're going to love this."

The walls in the living room were lined with sealed cardboard boxes. "You've boosted way more stuff than I thought. What's your secret?"

"Dip your cauldron as far upstream in the supply chain as you can."

"I'm actually going to write that down." I took out my notebook.

"Your thirty seconds have started."

I waved the wine. "Do you have glasses?"

"Is that a sock on your shoulder?"

"I don't understand the question."

"No. Really."

"I guess we can pass the bottle back and forth like hobos."

"It is a sock."

"OK. It is. My lucky sock."

She slit open one of the cardboard boxes and brought two crystal goblets chiming out of their wrapping. The bottle was only half full. I poured her most of it and sat on the couch. She kept standing. I played her the most recent message from George and asked if she thought we could trace it. She took George from me and cradled him in her shoulder like a telephone while draining her goblet.

I waited until the message was over. "That's a pizza arriving, right? So I'm thinking if we call all the pizza places in town we can find out who ordered it."

"You know how many pizza places there are in Plankton?"

"Like . . . four?"

"Infinity. But there's only one Mercy Pies. That's what they said at the end."

"I thought they said 'Jersey eyes.'"

"What would that even mean?"

"There you go again. Showing what a good team we are."

"'Team' implies I'm getting something out of this."

"You are! For it is in giving we receive. Don't you have something that can digitally read the file?"

"You have no idea what you're talking about, do you?"

"No."

"Stop and think. How many large mushrooms do you think they made at that exact time? You just need to get the address for the order. Which they'll never give you."

"Oh, I think they will."

She declined to be thanked with a kiss.

There was only one way to get what I needed from the manager of Mercy Pies. My least favorite way.

"I know you're getting ready for your shift. I want to give you eight hundred dollars for an address. Cash." We were standing inside the glass door I'd tapped on until he opened it. The amount made him close his mouth over whatever he was about to say.

"Your employees can't hear us. When I leave, take this napkin. There's four hundred dollars in there. I'll come back tonight with the other four hundred." Frank Boise thought he saved money by nickel-and-diming his dirty-work men, but you have to pay market rate for results. Market rate is the amount that makes people listen when you talk.

"What makes you think I can even get this address for you?"

"Because it's in your system. When someone calls you already know their address. The order was a large with mushrooms. The day and time are on a piece of paper on top of your new stack of twenties in this napkin. Bring the address to Skidoo's at one-thirty tonight." That was a bar three blocks away. "You close at midnight, so that should be plenty of time. If you have your crew clean as they go, you'll all get out of here a lot faster. Oh, and Larry?"

"My name is—"

"Let's go with Larry. Larry, no one will be harmed as a result of your cooperation." Even if he didn't believe that, it was prudent to throw a bone to his conscience. In case he had one.

Larry ended up bringing some "muscle" to the bar, a guy who still smelled like his shift and had an unconvincing sneer. There was some unpleasant business with a broken bottle. No permanent injury to either of them. I got the piece of paper with the address, and even paid them. Not the full amount. I withheld 380 dollars as a penalty for their hostility and distrust.

I was up early the next morning and standing outside the address, a four-story brick building on the downslope to Hello Bay, scrutinizing people as they emerged from it. I had a feeling I'd know him when I saw him, and I did. The same slumped shoulders, schlubby build, and duck-footed walk. I fell into step next to him.

"Good morning!"

"Do I know you?" he said.

It wasn't only his build that looked familiar. His face did, too. "On our way to work, are we?"

He took out a phone. "I'm calling the police."

"Alrighty, Whitey. I wouldn't mind talking to them myself."

He put the phone away. "Who are you?"

"Fucko."

"What?"

"I'm with Fucko. We've got a job for you. A real job, not whatever bullshit you're headed to now. Something commensurate with your talents. We've heard you're pretty much the best in town. Never mind that embarrassing incident the other day with Lito. How were you supposed to know he was already dead? At least you got away, right? All's well and all that."

"What—"

"Yes, we know about that. Haven't shared our info with the police yet. But let's not talk stick. Let's talk carrot." I shoved a napkin into his hands. "Here. Two hundred bucks. No, don't count it now!" God, are people dumb in this town. "There's a guy. You're going to scare him. That's it. Easy. Far below your skill level. That cash, that's just for starters." It was half of all the money I had. "Oh look, a coffee shop. I'm actually pretty coffee'd out, but it's hard to say no to another cup, you know what I mean?"

"I have to be at work in . . ."

I tightened my grip on his elbow. "I said it's hard to say no. I'll write a note for your boss. Do a good job with this thing and you won't need that job anyway." I got us a table and a couple of drips. He looked like he'd been shot out of a canon. "Sorry this is moving so fast. I got some more guys to line up before this thing goes down. You want a little authority in your cup?"

He shook his head at my flask.

"Here the guy's address."

"This is my address." I'd written it on the same paper Larry had surrendered from the floor of Skidoo's.

"Other side. Here's the keys."

"So what do you want me to—"

"Tell him you're gonna hurt him or kill him or whatever. That's all. Don't actually do anything." He put the paper and keys in a backpack nestled between his legs.

"So how will I know—"

I snatched up the backpack.

"I'd prefer if you not—"

"Kung fu manual! See, this is why we wanted you. You're not messing around, son."

He sat up straighter. "Kung fu is just an enhancement of my main practice."

"No doubt. Chung moo doe?"

He scoffed. "Ninjutsu."

I whistled. "I knew we made the right choice with you. You got all the belts and stuff?"

"Ninjutsu isn't about that."

"Say no more. What else do we have in here? A knife catalog, cool."

"Entry-level stuff. But it's amusing to see what's popular among amateurs."

"Right, I'd heard that about you, you're into some pretty esoteric"—I chopped the air—"*hai-ya*! and whatnot. You got one on you now, a knife? I know you do!"

He flushed a little and reached into his sock.

"Ankle sheath, holy shit. I'm going to have to get Fucko to double your rates. At least double." He handed me a folding knife that weighed nothing and sprang open noiselessly. "Beautiful piece!" I scraped the blade across the table. Every head swiveled toward the sound.

"That's a—could you please not—"

"How's the lock mechanism working for you?" The tip of the blade snapped off.

"That's a Damascus steel—"

"Looks like you got a fake. I just did you a favor. You know—" I lost my train of thought. I *had* seen him before, and not just at Lito's.

". . . a Damascus steel Ridge Master. It's only my walking-around knife, but it's still a very valuable—"

"Put it on the bill. Fucko will buy you ten of them. Listen, we need to clear the air about something.

Explain the Junko connection." He was the boyfriend in the photo. The one I saw at Junko's house right before she pulled her toy gun on me. Pete, was that what she'd called him?

He flinched. "How long have you been watching me?"

"You should be flattered Fucko thinks you're worth his time. They call your references when you got your last job? This is like that. Only you're going to be making more money now. A lot more."

He shifted in his seat. "What do you want to know?"

"How did you meet?"

"We were conversation partners."

"I have no idea what that means."

"I'm a Japanese learner. She's an English learner."

"Oh I get it. How did the Conversation Partner Association feel about that?"

"If we're wrong, gravity is wrong."

"Barf."

"I don't know if we can work together if you're going to—"

"You've gotta adjust to our style. What's the connection between Junko and Lito?"

"It's hard to say."

"Fucko needs to know what his people are into. It's a nonnegotiable point. Here's the part you're going to like though. You got any kind of problem with anyone in town and we'll take care of it. We don't want our people to have distractions when they're working for us. Besides, we already know you're a killer, Killer."

He looked at his coffee. "We wanted Ed. But Ed was dead."

"Mr. Cranberry, sure. We're familiar with him. So what'd he do besides fuck your girlfriend before you did?"

Pete started to stand up.

"Be glad I respect you enough to say it to your face."

He sat down.

"So you wanted to kill Ed but couldn't. Why was Lito your second choice?"

"Something happened to Junko."

"On Endorphin Island, we know. But what, exactly?"

"Junko doesn't want to go into details."

"Fair enough. Who got to Ed before you?"

"We don't know. Maybe a guy named Paul."

"Paul Dowell, TechCo. How did Junko know Paul?"

"Ed took her to a meeting of Paul's weird little club. She just wanted to practice her English."

"And they did something terrible to her. But Ed wasn't even there."

"He got her involved in that group."

"I see your point. So how did can't-kill-Ed become let's-kill-Lito?"

"This group of theirs. It was supposed to be something about investing. But there were all these sketchy people around."

"Like Lito."

"And some other guy with him. Big guy. We think they supplied the drugs Ed used on Junko."

"Sketchy people, shady things. Sounds like you did a thorough investigation."

He looked at his watch. "I really need to get going."

"We are currently paying you far more per hour for your natural talents than they are for you to be their bitch, but that's OK. We're friends now. I'll walk with you."

Outside, the sunrise continued its failure to do more than dilute the gray of the sky. Glass buildings rose on all sides to mirror the failure.

"Someone else got Ed, so you did your next-best-ninja duty and popped Lito. But why a gun, Ninja Pete? Shouldn't you have used a ninja technique?"

"I don't go by Ninja Pete."

"But it does have a ring to it, doesn't it?"

"Ninja technique is to use the best tools available to reach your goals."

"Good to know. But for this next job, we want you to go with a more traditional approach. No guns. Only your excellent martial arts skills."

"How will I know when it's time to do it?" We were now outside his crummy office building. I took the giraffe out of my bag and handed it to him. He jumped at the sight of it.

"I think you know George. And you know George's phone number, which you will now tell me. Keep him with you at all times until he tells you the secret go word."

Late-night eggs with Chang's men

I ARRIVED HOME TO the sound of someone moving around in my apartment. The manager changing the locks or someone else? I sat on the stairs and lit a cigarette and waited. A guy on his way down to take his dog to shit in the street said, "This is a nonsmoking building."

"I know, right?" B-Rays entered my chest and slowed everything down. At the tail end of my cigarette, the door to my apartment opened and a thick-set man emerged, pulling his jacket on and saying something to someone inside. He looked vaguely familiar but turned away before I could get a good look and walked down the hall. I reached for my lock-picking tools and remembered I had the key. I slipped it in the lock a sixteenth of an inch at a time, then opened the door and entered in one movement, putting me face-to-face with my sushi chef from the other night. He must have thought I was his friend coming back for his wallet or something because he sure was surprised. I bird-clawed his windpipe with one hand and clamped his balls with the other.

"Sorry about this. Really. Just sit down on the floor." He slid down the wall and crumpled. Rifling through his jacket I found a phone and a gun. "Were you planning to shoot me? Dozens of people would hear. What was your escape route?" He was a skinny hatchet-faced guy, panting and rubbing his neck. I offered him a hand. "You're OK. Your breathing is unobstructed. You'll have bruising. Nothing broken. Come on. Let's sit down over here." He was dazed but took my hand up and sat on the sofa.

"How do you even use one of these?" I was examining the gun. "All these slides and locks . . . seems more complicated than necessary." I sighted a coffee cup on the windowsill. "*Pew! Pew!* How do you take out the bullets?"

He was getting his breath back. "There . . . by the trigger . . ." I pushed where he said and a canister slid out and clattered onto the runway for the tiny airplane.

"Where did your friend go?"

"To get some food."

"There aren't very good options around here. Hopefully he finds the Thai place. I think they're still open. Does he have a gun, too?"

"No."

"Well of course you'd say that. Oh shit, is that him now?" A rattle at the door. I opened it to find the second chef from the other night. I pulled him in by his forearms. The first chef popped up from the sofa and fretted behind me. I two-stepped Chef Two next to his little buddy. He looked like a bulldog next to his hatchet-faced partner, who now opened his mouth.

"That!" I said to him. "That was the moment to make a move, right when he came in. It's too late now."

"There's two of us, even without a gun." Hatchet Face was breathing hard. Bulldog still looked disoriented.

"So why are you still talking? Go for it. I'll cut you open like a melon."

"I don't see any knife."

"And you never will." My hands hung loose by empty pockets. They looked at each other. Hatchet Face let his shoulders slump, then they both did.

"We didn't come here to fight."

"Glad to hear that. Because you're doing a shitty job of it. What's your name?" I nodded at Hatchet Face.

"Maurice."

I turned to Bulldog. "And you're . . . don't tell me. Mugsy." Mugsy shook his head. "No—"

"Mugsy it is. Maurice and Mugsy. Did you guys pick the lock?"

They nodded.

"Which one of you?"

Mugsy looked at Maurice.

"Nice job! Leaving to go get food though, that was bad. You should have brought some power bars or something. 'Impatience is the sin from which all other sins arise.' You ever hear that?"

I was losing them. "I'm not going to do anything to you. Unless you attack me. As I mentioned. So what was supposed to happen here?"

They sat.

"Your food is spilled all over. You want something to eat? Come to the kitchen so we can chat some more."

I got the pan going with olive oil and garlic. "You know what kind of day I've had? I've been stabbed by men, rejected by women, spit on by children. Then you guys. I just moved here, and I have to say, it's a pretty shitty little town you've got here. You want anything on your eggs? I'll just leave out the hot sauce and salt and you can do what you want."

I buttered the toast. "No offense, but you guys are really bad at your job. This can't be the only thing you do. I mean, in the criminal vein? I know you cut fish for your day jobs. And you seem to be great at that, by the way."

They were quiet. I pointed my butter knife at them. "What else do you do?"

"Move a little bit of drugs." They'd apparently settled between them that Maurice would do the talking.

"Sounds exciting." I put the plates on the table. "Maurice, would you say grace?"

His eyes bulged.

"Say it like your dad used to."

"Heavenly Father, we thank Thee for the sustenance we are about to receive and ask you to bless our souls with peace."

"That was nice. Was your dad a good guy?"

"A drunk."

"Oh well. Tell me something. Does being a sushi chef help you with your . . . other pursuits?"

They were quiet again.

"You're really making it hard to establish a conversational flow."

Maurice looked at his hands. "Um, I guess you develop a sense of people."

"I can see how you would. Let's go back to my first question. Then we can call it a night. What was supposed to happen here?"

"We were supposed to find out who you are and what you're doing."

"Not kill me?"

"Not necessarily."

"So I come through the door, you wave the gun, and I tell you my secrets?"

"Pretty much."

"Look, this is a little confusion between me and your boss. I actually work for him too. There's a lot you don't know. Let's go see him right now and clear it up. You got a car?"

Maurice nodded.

"You drive then. We'll clear this up and call it a night. No hard feelings on any side."

We walked to their station wagon a couple blocks away, them in front and me behind. It actually had the East Sea Sushi logo painted on the side.

"I know you're proud of where you work, but you might want to rethink your getaway-vehicle strategy next time." I sat in back. "So how did you hook up with the big man?"

"Through Lito," said Maurice.

"So why did you kill Lito?"

"Lito? We didn't kill Lito!" Maurice turned around in his seat to say this. Mugsy was driving.

"Huh, I almost believe you. Who killed him then?"

"We don't know."

"Is this where he lives?" Mugsy was backing up into a space on a dark street in Trapper's Yard. A few blocks from Boise's office. We got out. As if in response to a radio signal, they took off running at the same time, Maurice in long, loping strides, Mugsy in frantic little bulldog steps next to him.

I gimp-stepped far behind. "Hey, you fucks, I gave you eggs!" They dissolved into the dark. I gasped for air and contemplated another walk home.

Bound to the mast

"So they took off."

"Yeah."

"And you didn't catch them."

"I couldn't keep up."

I'd lured Brenda out of her depression chamber for a walk around What Lake. Two couples jogged by in formation. Creepy as fuck. Whatever happened to cocktails and adultery? I wore my ball cap and sunglasses in case we ran into Paul Dowell or his bathrobe neighbors.

"I'm acquainted with your stamina."

"Uncalled for."

"What were you going to do if you'd managed to get inside the boss person's place?"

"Improvise. I think I know who it is."

"You really are determined to get dead, aren't you?"

"You sound like you care. I meant to tell you that you look particularly nice today. Those sunglasses give a real flair to your hostility."

"If only you were as charming as you are in your own mind."

"I'm serious! I value your perspective. I would thumbtack my dick to a cake that had that written on it."

"What?"

"You don't get the reference? It's from a poem."

"No it isn't."

"Look, I know you're kind of a . . . how do you say it? A basket case. And I've been selfish and intrusive."

"Are you giving a speech?"

"I also know you're not a real criminal. You haven't even tried to move any of that stuff piled up at your place. You're a klepto."

"Not your business."

"There's no shame in that. But you might consider monetizing if you're stealing anyway. You obviously have a knack for it."

"Are you trying to mentor me in crime?"

"Friendly advice is all."

"I don't think I can do this, Pope."

"Do what? We're not doing anything."

"You're pressuring me with your friendly attitude."

"Look, I get it. That you occasionally turn into a smoldering pile of hatred for everyone and everything. I'm not trying to deprive you of that. I just like you, OK?"

"Are we negotiating a contract here?"

"Yes. Sulk off to be a hateful little lunatic from time to time. I'll be here when you come out again. I don't have anything else going on right now."

"And I thought romance was dead."

"You won't even let me agree with you."

"I thought you'd never catch on. Oh, by the way, I call bullshit on your story about the insurance settlement and the bus running over your foot."

"Whaaat? Come on."

"You don't even have a checking account."

"How did—"

"You're not the only one capable of basic recon. You're stuck up, Pope. You don't think you are, but you are. And you have no checking account, and you're not getting insurance money."

"They send cashier's checks."

"Stop, you're embarrassing yourself."

"So you're not the only one who holds things back."

"And those friends of yours that ran you out of town, and the girl. You're leaving a whole lot out of that story."

"I left them, and took some cash with me. Not much, but enough to make them very mad. That's all."

"Huh. So how many people are you fucking right now?"

"Can I still count you?"

"Let's say yes. For the moment."

"One."

"Keep it that way or it'll be zero."

"So we're friends?"

"Paddle me back home and don't call me again until next week. Then I'll consider being your friend."

Two lake crossings and one bike ride later, I arrived home to find my stuff wasn't yet tossed on the sidewalk, but someone inside had turned the radio on. I went in. Anyone dangerous would've at least tried to be quiet.

"Remember that lock-picking lesson you gave me?"

And just like that, Lisa was back in my life. She emerged from the bathroom wearing my robe and drying her hair.

"No."

"Me either. I got the manager to let me in."

"Haven't lost your powers of persuasion."

"Come here, Pope."

I followed her into my bedroom.

"I came here to return something to you. Lie down. Remember these?" Her head cocked, she stood in my robe, which was coming open, and dangled a pair of handcuffs on an outstretched finger.

"I remember trying them out once. My heart wasn't in it though. That's what you said, anyway."

"It wasn't."

"Was I supposed to hit you? I guess the procedure was unclear to me."

She cuffed my wrists to the headboard. "There isn't always a procedure, Pope."

She took my shoes off, then my pants and boxers. Shirt and socks but no pants—it's not a dignified look. She wasn't looking at me though. She was in the next room, getting a beer out of the fridge. I'd been home for ninety seconds.

"Do you have any weed?"

"In the leather pouch on the table"

"Leather pouch, mystical. Do you keep your eighteen-sided dice in there, too?"

"Yes. Yes, I do." I was having trouble keeping up my end of the conversation. The air currents on my cock were suddenly intense.

She was back, straddling me, the robe completely open now. "Hold that for me." She put the beer in my hands, and I held it between my palms. "Don't drop it." She lit my pipe and worked the carb with her thumb, my cock now brushing her abdomen.

"I knew you'd leave me." She put the pipe aside and leaned forward to take the beer from me. She pressed her breasts against my face, then sat back again and regarded me as a bird would a worm. "No man ever left me before, Pope. They're all cocky at first, but then they get hooked and start mooning and pining. But you did it."

"That's strange, I don't remember leaving you." My voice sounded far off.

She took a swig of my beer, turning her head to the side to maintain eye contact.

"You think maybe I could have a sip of that?" My mouth was very dry.

"Yeah, I don't think so."

"I didn't leave you, Lisa."

"Well, anyway you left. I thought you didn't give a fuck."

"Sorry to disappoint you."

"No note, nothing, just gone." She was distractedly rubbing the beer bottle against my cock.

"I was going to leave a note." My voice was a whisper.

"I wouldn't be here if you had." She dropped the bottle on the floor.

"Just go ahead and put that anywhere."

She rolled a condom over my cock and leaned forward to speak into my ear. "I'm going to ride you for a while." She impaled herself and began to rock. She fucked slowly, propping herself on my shoulders.

"You missed this, didn't you?" she breathed into my ear.

Yes. The answer to that, if I could've gotten one out, was yes. She slipped off and turned around and started bouncing her ass up and down on me. She was louder now, fingering her clit and gripping me with her thighs for balance. She fucked herself with my cock until she came and collapsed next to me.

"Glad to see me?"

"I haven't really had an opportunity to gather my thoughts. Can you unlock me?"

"Maybe in a bit." She propped herself up on an elbow and ran her hand under my shirt and found the wound on my shoulder. "I see you've been making new friends."

"How are my old friends doing?"

"I came all the way across the country and you want to talk about them?"

"You're right. Fuck those guys."

"They're shitty. You should see what they've been getting into. Mugging people who are taking out their garbage. Drugs. Dog hunting. Getting terrible haircuts."

"What kind of drugs?"

"Coke? Meth? Whatever comes in those little bags."

"Selling or using?"

"Selling was the theory, but that didn't last. Banh is intolerable now."

"Wait, did you say dog hunting? I don't get the angle."

"There is no angle. They like hunting dogs. Also, they've been stealing tools from tool rental trucks."

"That's the only good one I've heard so far. Easy to sell, hard to trace."

"So what kind of shit are you pulling, Pope?"

"Nothing to speak of. How's little whatshisname?" I probably forgot to mention that Lisa is a mom. She's not good at it.

"The same. Bigger," she said.

"So you decided to take a little trip to see me."

"I wanted to thank you for leaving me."

"Your husband helped make the decision a little easier with what he did to my foot."

I should probably mention that when I said "a bus ran over my foot," I meant something more along the lines of "my former friends tried to kill me with a crowbar." Banh is Lisa's husband. I probably forgot to mention that, too.

"You know I could have destroyed them after that," I said.

"Sure, Pope. I'm not doubting your manly ability to locate a gun and shoot people. But you didn't. You took off."

"My hands are starting to fall asleep."

"OK, I'll let you go. You're going to have to earn it first by paying a little more homage to *mon* clit."

"What?"

She shimmied up my body and clapped her thighs around my face. "I seem to remember that you were pretty good at this. If you want to breathe again, you better come through."

I don't know how long it took me to get her off. Time is different in Pussy World. She eventually toppled off me.

"Oh God, oh yes. OK, you've earned your freedom." She unlocked me and I massaged blood back into my hands. Her limbs flopped over my bed like she'd lost all muscle power. "There's something else I need to tell you," she said to the ceiling. "About why I'm here."

"I thought you just dropped in to return my handcuffs. And to thank me for leaving you."

"They're here, too. In town. Banh and the boys."

I sat up. "Fuck! Do they know where I am?"

"No. I haven't told them yet."

"Yet?"

"Well, I need to kick-start this thing, Pope. This showdown." She pantomimed shooting guns in the air. "Or whatever's going to happen. You think I want to stick around here forever? We've got to get this over with one way or another."

"What the fuck is wrong with you?"

"Jesus, you really are tense. I'm sure you'll come up with something. You're good in these situations, Pope. You should give yourself a little more credit. They're not in your league, Pope. They can't hurt you."

"They've actually done a fairly decent job of hurting me. So what are your plans while you decide when to tell them about me?"

"I dunno, are there any cute guys in this town?"

"No."

"Well, whatever happens, those guys are headed for a fall. They haven't been bringing in any money for ages, and I expect they'll all be either dead or in jail pretty soon. Even if they do succeed in taking you out. Which is all they care about. The worse things have gone for them, the more they're obsessed with you. You should be flattered. They're so doped out and deluded they think killing you will somehow instantly get them the giant wad of cash they assume you have. You don't happen to have a giant wad of cash, do you?" She was talking to the ceiling again.

"I do not."

"Anyway, I suppose I'll have to get a job or something after this is over. So this is sort of a vacation before that happens. I'm also curious to see how it plays out. It should be good."

"It's great to have you in my corner."

"Oh, but I am! I'll be rooting for you. Obviously. Don't look so glum. Are you still sulking about the end of our little fling? Come on, we were fucking, then we weren't. How bad could it be?"

"It was like having molten lead poured down my throat."

She burst out laughing. "You would really be a lot happier if you weren't so melodramatic." She rolled over and presented her ass. "Don't like me leaving, do you? I'm all yours for as long as you can pin me down with your cock."

Some daytime movements

THE PHONE RANG. I let it.

Lisa was gone. Despite my best efforts, I eventually had to let her up. The Riders were in town somewhere, probably on amphetamines. I wasn't going to throw myself in their direction just yet. Don't give an opponent energy they don't already have. I was going to have to write that down in my little notebook. But why would they call me? They wouldn't. I picked up the phone on the fifth ring.

"This is Frank Boise."

"No shit, really?" I sat up straighter.

"What the fuck are you doing going around telling people you're me?"

"Wait, how did you get my number?"

"You filled out a job application, dipshit."

"Point taken. So the whole pretending-to-be-you thing. I stopped doing it. And I apologize. Is there anything further I can help you with at this point?"

He gave me some suggestions. I let him get to the end of his list.

"OK, Frank. I won't try to dispute any of that. You're right to be mad. You have A RIGHT to be mad. I would be, too. That reminds me, did you send any-one after me?"

"After you?"

"With a gun."

"Because of this dumb shit you think I'm going to have you KILLED?"

"No, you're right. That makes no sense. But what about the original thing you asked me to do, Frank? The red hat, Maurice, what was all that, Frank?"

"Stop saying my name like a goddamn car sales-man. What I do is none of your good goddamn business."

"You swear like a grandpa, Frank. No, wait, don't hang up. Please, one other thing. Who do you think killed Ed Cranberry?"

"You ignorant child. It's got nothing to do with you."

"Can I confess something? I didn't like you at first. But by not stabbing, punching, or calling the cops on me, you're moving up my list. This call has actually made me like you *more*, Frank. You've got pep, Frank."

Frank described what my opinion meant to him.

"Frank, can you just forget for one second about how mad you are? I've got a proposition for you."

I had a second proposition, this one for Maurice and Mugsy.

It was just before the lunch shift. I lingered in the hall by the employee entrance to East Sea Sushi until the redheaded busboy appeared. I tailgated him through the door.

"Hey, sorry, I can't let you—"

I pushed past him. "Tatsu will thank you. He's meeting me here."

I sat down at the sushi bar. Mugsy and Maurice jumped about a mile when they saw me, but just as quickly realized that if there was an upper hand, they had it.

"We can call the cops." Maurice still spoke for them.

"Come on, fellas. You broke into MY house, and you want to call the cops on ME? Because I sat down at your sushi bar? I know you work for a total amateur, but have some pride. Look how beautiful your display case is. I'm not blind. I can see when a guy knows his way around a slab of, what is that, *maguro*?"

Maurice looked down at the hunk of red flesh behind the glass among the other offerings of the day. Egg omelet, white fish, octopus. Mugsy contemplated the bowl of shrimp he'd just been shelling with swift, automatic movements.

Maurice said, "It's *chutoro*."

"That's what I'm talking about. Who even knows what that means? You're craftsmen. This has got to bother you a little, right? The way this is being done?"

They had no response to that.

"What did I ever do to you except defend my home without injuring you in any way? I mean other than your throat, Maurice. Sorry about that. All I wanted was to talk. And that's still all I want."

They looked around.

"No one can hear us," I said. "Red's emptying the recycling."

Mugsy absently shelled a few more shrimp.

"There's only two things I need to know. Then I'll disappear forever. First, who killed Ed Cranberry?"

Maurice looked around again, decided *fuck it*, and said, "Lito."

"I doubt that, but go on."

"Everyone knew."

"Who's everyone?"

"Clarence, everyone."

"Mugsy, did you know your name tag says 'Jesus'? That's just confusing. Why would Lito kill Ed?"

They went quiet again. Then Maurice said, "There's a lot we don't know."

"I'll say."

"But there's a guy named Paul. He had some kind of club. He wanted to get into selling drugs. With Clarence."

"Sounds good so far."

"And Ed had a problem. With Paul and Clarence. We don't know what."

"And Lito?"

"He wanted to impress Clarence by taking care of it himself."

"Let's say that's all true. Who killed Lito?"

"We don't know."

"No? OK, now about Clarence. I need to talk to him."

"You said you worked for him."

"Which was a lie. Obviously. Are we really going to get hung up on that? Jesus, if that *is* your name, why is everyone so bad at conversation in this town? If you only knew what I've gone through just to TALK to people here. We can meet wherever Clarence wants. You can be there. He can bring his mommy to hold his wee-wee. Or maybe that's your job. You fuck your boss, Mugsy?"

"He'll find you."

Mugsy spoke for the first time. Whatever he thought was going to happen when Clarence found me, it was making him smile.

Tatsu appeared. He was holding an aluminum baseball bat.

"That's a good look for you, Senator. Chefs always think they're tough, but I think you really might be."

He moved toward me. I didn't get up.

"Your plan is to assault me in your own restaurant? In view of your employees?"

He looked at Maurice and Mugsy.

"Not them," I said. "Them."

A couple of servers in their black-and-whites smoking on the parking-garage roof across the street were looking our way.

"Still, I can in fact take a hint, despite appearances. *Irasshaimase!* The opposite of that is what you're saying to me, am I right?" I crossed the floor and pressed on the heavy crossbar handle and let myself out.

The key to my place still worked. For once I had no company. I barricaded the door with my sofa and went down for a nap. Hard. The bed still smelled like Lisa. From deep in a black hole, I heard knocking. I got myself to the door. "Yeah?"

"It's me, you idiot."

I pushed the sofa aside and opened the door and the red cowboy hat reentered my life on Brenda's head.

"Hey, wow, I'm glad you're here." I was suddenly very awake. "You look like a million bucks." Under the hat she was for some reason back to her TechCo look. Black dress, stockings, lipstick.

"You going to invite me in?"

"God, please. Come in."

"I've decided we can go back to sleeping together. When I feel like it."

"Part-Time Dick Boy is my actual middle name."

She went into the bedroom and stopped.

"I probably should have cleaned that up." Three shriveled condoms were on the floor next to the bed.

"Those . . . this is kind of funny . . . I don't have any good words here."

"Give it a shot. The first words that come to your mind."

"Look, you didn't seem to want—"

"Right. Got it."

"Do you want to hit me in the face?"

"I would, but that might actually make you feel better. And I don't want that."

"Since it's possible I'll never see you again, can I ask one last thing?"

"No."

"Can I stay with you? I'm guessing no. This place isn't going to be available to me after . . . OK, I'm getting a definite *no* vibe from you right now. It's fine. I'm sure I'll work something out."

"You lookin'?"

The Denim Queen was on her usual perch atop Yick Fung Overlook. I wondered if she was familiar with any of the other standard human greetings.

"No, a bit low on funds at the moment. I just wanted to ask you something."

She was gazing at the horizon like the pagoda gazebo on the hill was the deck of a tall ship. "Yeah?"

"You ever see people sleep in this park at night?"

More noble gazing. "Nah."

"Think it's a safe place to sleep?"

She blew smoke at the clouds. "The tweakers don't come around here at night. They're all in the Jungle." That's what they called the homeless encampment in the woods off the highway. She nodded at a cement wall. "You sleep on the other side of that, it'd keep the wind off and nobody'd see you."

"Thanks. Just exploring some options. That's very helpful."

"Hey." She called to my back.

"Yeah?"

She was holding out six cigarettes and a joint. "Here, on the house."

"That's really very generous of you. I appreciate it."

She gave no sign of having heard me. She was back to scanning for storms.

The big smashup

"Y ou ran off like a bitch." Banh had me. It was the first of several mistakes to go back to my apartment. He'd emerged from a dark alley and was now waving a gun around as he talked.

"If you mean in the manner of a female dog," I said, "many breeds run with great dignity."

"No one ever thought you were funny, Pope." The gun was an accessory for his bad-guy outfit.

"If I don't get a chance to mention it before you kill me, I want to tell you how much I like your ensemble. Is that lambskin? You still look like the cunt of a hairless rat though."

He swiped the gun across my face and opened up a gash in that little crevice where nose meets cheek.

Provoking Banh into hitting me didn't do any good. No witnesses. And no time to focus and catch B-Rays. If I hadn't gone past the alley, I'd have been home already. Yes, I'd have run into the other two Riders waiting in my room. But those guys had never been hard to handle.

I accepted Banh's invitation to step into his car, parked deep in the alley. We sat in the front seat. His face gleamed in the green backlight of the dashboard. I held a sleeve to my gash. "Nice choice on the wheels, too. Flashy model, out-of-state plates, great choices for this kind of activity."

"You want me to kill you now?"

"Definitely not. If I get a vote, I'm going with no."

"You ran off like a bitch, and you're going to die like a bitch."

"'Ran off.' That's the wrong way to look at it."

"That's what happened."

"I withdrew. As a kindness to all of us."

"Right. You're fucking Gandhi."

What actually happened was, right before I left town, Banh and the other two Riders—the ones currently draining my bourbon—had surprised me getting out of my car. They did some punching. It wasn't great punching, but good enough. Then they did some kicking when I was down. They would have broken more than a blood vessel in my eye if they'd worn boots instead of mesh running shoes. Never thinking ahead, that was them. Banh did at least bring a crowbar. It occurred to me when I saw it that I was going to die the same way as that kid my brother killed. Skull broken. His helmet, the cop called it. Brains and blood on the pavement, staring at nothing. But they had no contingency plan for witnesses, so a guy walking his tiny dog froze them. Banh hesitated with the crowbar, then right before they took off, the dog walker sprawled in their wake, he brought it down on my foot.

This incident convinced me my friends were mad at me. Their execution had been inept but highly enthusiastic. I further surmised they would continue being mad at me until I gave them money or they killed me. Or I killed them. Which would have been a piece of cake. Every part of it—getting the gun, following their drunk asses around for a few days, choosing a good time and an escape plan that took into account the average police response time for that part of town. Probably daytime, when the city flowed with people and traffic to blend into. Close range, no missing. Three brains, three hearts, six bullets.

I didn't come to Plankton to escape them. I came to escape myself. And because Banh's wife broke my heart.

"Pretty much, yeah. I'm Gandhi."

"That your fag hat?"

I'd taken to a tweed bucket hat from the thrift store. "Yes, my fag hat. I'm a fag. Good thing Lisa is so open minded."

He hit me again with his gun, opening a cut on the other side of my nose. I took my shirt off and pressed it to both wounds. I felt my teeth with my tongue. Everything seemed to be in place. I breathed deep to open my lungs like a sail to any passing B-Rays.

"Interesting approach with the gun. The slashing motion. I would've expected more of a blunt-force angle."

"You know I'm looking for reasons not to kill you, right?"

"No, you just said you *were* going to kill me. You don't have anywhere to go now, threat-wise. But I doubt you'll do it here. In your own car."

"Yeah, Professor. Thanks for your concern. Surprisingly, we've done OK without your oversight."

"And you probably have more fun, too, right? Every night is pizza night and you can stay up as late as you want?"

"You really want me to shoot, don't you?"

"No. But if you do, and you're bending over to hear my last words—maybe I'll share a final tender memory of our friendship, like the alley walk—you're going to hear it through a lot of gurgling. Internal bleeding. That's how torso shots kill you. Shooting me in the head would be instant. Probably. But then there'd be the brain geyser on your white-leather interior."

The tender memory I was talking about was this time we walked backward through an alley in a strange part of town in the middle of the night, tripping balls, fearless.

"Wow, yu're really forcing me to confront the visceral horror of gun violence right now.

"You were never as dumb as I thought. Aren't you drunk? I assumed you were drunk."

"There is one thing you can do to save yourself."

"There's no money, Banh."

Banh and me started doing break-ins as another way to get high. Doing bad shit was an intoxicant. We were tight then, some of those druggy mornings, the pink cirrus skies a splatter portrait of our shared brain patterns. The other two guys followed our lead. They laughed when we did and went where we said to go.

We went through windows and back doors, made silent single-file processions between ventilation towers on strip-mall rooftops. We passed bulging duffel bags from hand to hand and into trunks and back seats. We shared cigarettes over a banquet of all the booty a midsize town in the middle of the country has to offer. Cases of liquor. Jewelry. Coin collections. Electronics virginal in their original boxes, the holographic seals catnip to fences. And sweetest of all, unruly piles of other people's cash.

A city's cash sinks at night into safes at the end of hallways studded with security cams. To get cash, you have to do daytime holdups. Which I hated. That's why I drifted away. The bank job I did with the getaway apartment was a last effort to keep us together. I still liked them some of the time. But if we were going to do holdups, I thought we should work out a system.

They were partly right about the money from the bank job. I'd kept more of it than was warranted by a strict reading of our agreement. That wasn't the point though. I'd found a successful method to get at the cash the other three had decided was our goal. But it wasn't going to work. The lady who said she was thinking about her kid when I pointed a gun at her—that killed the whole idea for me.

"How can there be no money?" said Banh through green lips.

"There wasn't much to begin with. Maybe three grand."

"You said eight."

"I wanted to win the bet."

"You wanted to fuck my wife."

I didn't think it would be productive to tell him that Lisa had taken the initiative on that front.

Lisa. She arrived one day with the usual crowd that came to our place to get high and was always around after that. She slid seamlessly into being Banh's girlfriend. That's when Banh starting going alpha. The other two Riders fell in with it. It did have a logic. The one who wins the female is dominant.

Not that there weren't other women around. But Lisa was *the* woman. The one with the gifted hips, the one who made every man sit up straighter as she sailed through the room on waves of her own laughter. I don't know why she gravitated to Banh. Her jokes went over his head. She'd smirk at me when they did. I held her gaze and made her look away first. She called my bluff and things got going while I was prepping for the bank job. We made fuck puddles all over the getaway apartment.

"She was never going to leave me and Junior," said Banh. They'd named their stupid kid Banh Junior. "You don't understand her, Pope. She's conventional under it all. Worries what people will think. She'd never be seen with you."

"Harsh words from a rat cunt."

He was too taken with his theme to go for the bait. "You know why Lisa got sick of you? You're a crybaby. You were never a brother to us." Waving his gun at my crotch, he said, "Your dick bigger than mine?"

I think he actually was drunk. "Probably, yeah."

For some reason this opinion only gave him a far-off look. "Did you know we had to kill someone recently?"

"I'm not surprised. You're a bad dude now, Banh. You do bad stuff."

"So what bullshit are you involved in here?"

I caught a sudden gust of B-Rays. "Banh, you would not believe this place. Even a pack of idiots like you guys could run rings around the people here. Remember those alarm systems with the magnets on the windows? They still use those."

"Serious?"

"You can basically do whatever you want. I even did a daytime break-in the other day. In, out, gone."

"Residential?"

"Yeah. There's a kind of head criminal here. He sent a couple of guys to scare me the other night. You wouldn't believe who. Sushi chefs."

"They do jobs between lunch and dinner?" Banh settled back a little in his buttery lambskin, though his gun barrel remained a steadily hovering black hole.

My oxford was getting saturated with the blood from my two gashes. I shifted it around to get fresh fabric on them. "Right? And they have one gun between them. They were waiting for me in my place. Only they ran off before they did anything."

"Just like you."

"Right, yeah. Good one."

And then he arrived. I'd expected him, just not at that exact moment.

Thick air

I T WAS CLARENCE, aka Chang, aka Charles, that big-ass coworker of Lito's I'd met on the first tier of Mayfern Cranberry's three-tiered front yard. This was a city where kingpins prune trees. I was cresting the pinnacle of the local criminal establishment.

He was under a street light in the mouth of the alley, his shoulders and big hands unmistakable. I reached over and flashed the headlights on and off, making him turn sharply our way.

"You motherfucker," said Banh, swinging his gun to me, then stopping as he saw Clarence closing on the driver's side. Banh lowered the window. "How about you get lost, Chief."

Clarence didn't say anything because there was nothing to say. He looked in, saw me, saw the gun pointed at me, and put his paw over it. Banh opened his mouth to say something. Pocketing the gun with one hand, Clarence grabbed Banh's throat with the other and squeezed until the veins stood out in his forearm. Banh's face looked like an over-ripe tomato.

I took Banh's phone from the dash and got out of the car. I dialed a number, waited for the beep, and said, "Go." Then I went around to the other side of the car, where Clarence was busy choking Banh. In addition to being taller and stronger than me, Clarence was the first guy I'd met in Plankton who seemed to know what he was doing. And Banh had been about to kill me. But watching a man choke another man to death is not stylish.

When I stepped toward Clarence he was already stepping toward me, and already had the gun out. Was Banh dead? Sure looked like it, his head lolled back and motionless.

"Let's go in," said Clarence.

"You know, you're the second guy to point that gun at me tonight?" I was still holding the oxford to my face.

He pushed the gun to the back of my head. "You're nothing." He took a fistful of hair and used it as a handle to walk me toward the entrance.

Christ, where were the witnesses? Whose ass do you have to eat in this town to get the cops called? Clarence took my keys from my pocket. We went through the front door, through the lobby, past the manager's office. No sign of him now that some actual shit was going down in his building.

There was a new eviction notice on my door to replace the one I'd wiped my ass with. Clarence made a lot of noise getting the door open. It didn't help anything though. The other two Riders were slow as always. I can't avoid telling you their names at this point. Paul and Pete. I know that's confusing. I'll call them Rider Paul and Rider Pete to distinguish them from Paul Dowell, TechCo, and Ninja Pete.

They looked up with cow faces. They'd smashed the place up. There were letters smeared in brown on my wall, and a smell to match.

I held the bloody oxford around my mouth like a wreath and talked through the hole. "Paul, Pete. Great to see you. This man is going to kill us all. Writing 'Pope Fag' on my wall with your own shit will now have been the last thing you did on earth."

"Who are . . .? What . . .?"

"Rest your brains," I said.

Clarence waved me onto the sofa next to them. "Who are they?" he said. I didn't like how calm he was.

"This here's my life coach Pete and Pete's life coach Paul."

His face didn't move.

"No, but seriously, their names really are Pete and Paul. They came to kill me, same as you."

Pete spit out, "That's right! We've got nothing against you. We don't like him either."

I thought of something. "How did you guys get in? Did you finally learn how to pick locks?"

"Got a dupe from your girlfriend."

"Brenda?"

"Who's Brenda? Lisa, dickwaffle."

"Sorry, Clarence, I know it's annoying when people talk about friends you don't know. Just let us get caught up real quick. Paul and Peter, Banh is dead. I don't have any money. I don't believe Lisa gave you a key. OK, I think that covers it."

Clarence said, "Why were you bothering Paul?"

"He's talking about a different Paul," I told Rider Pete and Rider Paul.

"What do you mean Banh is dead?" said Rider Paul.

"Shut the fuck up!" said Clarence.

"We need an agenda. How about we cover the Banh thing first? Yes, to reiterate, Banh is dead. Clarence here strangled him. Now, Clarence, your question was about what I did to Paul—different Paul," I reminded the Riders.

Pete leaped up. "The goddamn fucking—"

"It's a lot to take in, but we're on the second agenda item." I oscillated my bloody wreath to address everyone equally. "Clarence wants to know what his sushi chef friends couldn't get out of me the other night."

Clarence waited for me to shut up. "What did you want with Paul?"

"One, to confirm he's a rapist shitbag who deserves death. He is. Two, to find out who killed Lito. He says you."

Clarence didn't react to any of that.

"What the fuck did you do to Banh? I'm going to—" Pete was starting to hyperventilate.

"If you don't make them stop talking, I'm going to kill you all." Clarence wasn't mad, just sharing information.

"Go for it. I'd start with them though."

"Hey!" said Rider Pete.

"He said shut up, man!" said Rider Paul to Rider Pete.

"You two, stand up, and face the other way. No more talking."

Pete and Paul rose on wobbly legs and turned to the window.

"And you," he said to me, "put those on." He'd spotted the handcuffs Lisa had left behind.

"These don't actually work—"

He pulled my arms behind my back and got the cuffs on, making me drop my bloody shirt. "Now don't say anything else except what I ask you."

"Roger, Clarence." I could feel a warm trickle from my two face wounds onto my chest.

"Someone harvested a smiley face into my marijuana field. What does that mean?"

Whatever I'd expected him to say, it wasn't that. "Clarence, I'm afraid you lost me."

"Something happened to my crop."

"And you think I did it?"

"Not really, but it seems like something you would do."

"I admit that's true."

The door opened. Banh. He had a gun. It went off at the same time as Banh's other gun in Clarence's hand. They both stood still, then Clarence collapsed.

"Banh! Jesus!" said Rider Pete, skilled as ever at summing up current events. Clarence was making a gurgling sound on the floor.

I said, "Banh, how about you and your buddies get out of here. You might not have killed him. I'll call an ambulance."

Banh didn't look like the seasoned killer he'd been at the beginning of our evening together. His face was white and his throat was blue.

"Banh, look at me. You're going into shock. You gotta leave. Take these idiots. Leave your car. You can come back for it later."

Riders Paul and Pete were enthusiastic. "You heard him, let's get the fuck out of here."

Banh said, "We don't take the car, how do we get out of here?"

"There's a ring of skeletons in my jacket there. Get yourself something on the street."

"What will you tell the cops?"

"Some bullshit. You know I'm good at that part."

"And you and me?"

"You're leaving me with this. Let's call it even."

Banh opened his mouth to agree when the door rattled and Ninja Pete skittered in. He was wearing some kind of martial arts jacket. He struck a stance in the doorway.

"The fuck?"

"Don't shoot him, Banh!"

Banh turned the gun back on me, now snapped out of his trauma trance. "You're the boss again, are you? That's over, Pope."

Ninja Pete produced a ninja star and threw it at Banh. It missed widely. Banh turned back to him.

"The fuck?"

Ninja Pete squared himself up like he was remembering the correct stance from ninja class and threw a second star with a twist of his hips that spasmed energy through his elbow and into his wrist. It whistled into Banh's forearm and embedded itself up to the special little ninja symbol in the middle.

The gun fell at Banh's feet as he shouted different combinations of *Jesus, fuck,* and *shit,* and Ninja Pete stood motionless in a birdlike post-throw pose. I threw myself faceup over the gun and fumbled for it with my cuffed hands. Rider Pete and Rider Paul rushed me as I kicked spastically at the floor to propel myself toward Ninja Pete.

"Take it, take it!" I turned onto my stomach to get the gun to him. He broke his pose in time to dive for the gun as Rider Pete and Rider Paul also landed on top of me.

I was now pinned under the weight of three full-grown dumbasses.

Ninja Pete did some martial arts shouting at his opponents. *Ha! Ho!* That kind of thing. The other two were swearing and threatening. I couldn't tell whose hands were prying my fingers off the gun. "Do you have it?" I gasped to Ninja Pete, who was still going *Ha!*

He did have it. All three rolled off me, and I rolled over to find him pointing it at them. I pushed my face against the sofa to get myself to my feet. Banh, Rider Pete, and Rider Paul regarded me and Ninja Pete across two red blots in the rug where my face had been mashed into it. Me, shirtless, cuffed, and smeared with blood, and Ninja Pete holding the gun like one of the models in his military supplies catalog. The Riders stood still, then poured wordlessly out the door.

I heard Rider Pete's voice receding down the hallway. "Shit, we should have gone for the other guy's gun."

The cops

LONG STORY LONG, we'd made enough racket to finally attract the Plankton PD. It was their lucky day. What an amazing assembly of fine criminal talent to scoop up at once. Me, Ninja Pete, and Clarence, who was loaded into an ambulance by shouting medics. And Banh. The Riders had split up outside my door, and Pete and Paul got away.

I was given a quick patch-up in a second ambulance and handed back to the cops. Someone gave me a T-shirt. It said Cheeseburger Night. They cut off the handcuffs I was wearing and put on their own.

The Plankton police station was nice. Lots of wood and glass, high ceilings. Way nicer than the one in Dayton, which was freezing and had puddles in the hallway. I tried to tell the cop about that, but he wasn't interested. That was something all cops shared. They weren't interested in my little observations.

The cop assigned to me had a square head. He looked tired. "You've made quite a name for yourself as a sushi customer."

"Tell me more."

"Wanna see some video from East Sea Sushi?"

"You want to talk about that instead of what happened tonight?"

"No. Who's the guy who got shot?"

"Someone who came to see me."

"How did you know him?"

"I don't."

"Then three more guys show up."

"Two, three, I don't remember."

"And someone from this group shoots the first guy."

"You're really nailing this so far."

"They smear shit on your walls and handcuff you."

"Exactly."

"And then another stranger arrives, also for no reason, and throws a martial arts projectile at the guy with the gun."

"I'm pretty sure you don't need me here at all. Your grasp of events is excellent."

"And the guy who threw the projectile, what did he look like?"

"He was dressed in a ninja outfit."

"White?"

"Didn't I just say he was in a ninja outfit?" I'd gorged on B-Rays in the squad car.

The cop looked at the ceiling. "What if I told you that your friend in the hospital was awake and what he's saying doesn't match what you're saying?"

"I can't control what other people say."

"Let's say he says you're the shooter."

"I don't think that guy is saying anything. Banh got him square in the torso."

"You just called him Banh. I thought you didn't know him."

"Oh, I knew him once, but I certainly don't know what he's become. That's what I meant."

"I don't like you."

"And you want to scare me into testifying against Banh. Don't bother. I'll do it. I'll say whatever you want. You'll love him. Out-of-town perp, a record. He's perfect."

They kept me overnight. My public defender finally showed up. Tall guy in a windbreaker, fuming about procedure. I took his card and told him it would be OK.

East Sea Sushi wanted to press charges. I was told to stick around for that. As if I would ever want to leave Plankton. They seemed not to have connected me with the thing at Paul Dowell's house.

I signed everything they wanted me to and was waiting in one last room when the square-headed cop came in and smashed the back of my head with his flashlight.

"Let me give you some advice," he said. "Don't ever walk out of here like you got the better of us."

"Thanks for the advice," I said, memorizing his face.

I went back to my apartment in case by some miracle they hadn't changed the locks yet. They had. There was also crime tape across the doorframe, which I thought was a bit melodramatic. I picked the lock, packed some things in my bicycle bag, and set a course to the Gospel Mission Shelter.

The first of many drinks I bummed

NINJA PETE SURPRISED me again. This time by tracking me to the shelter one morning. "I think I might cop to a lesser and squeal." He wanted to talk strategy, one tough guy to another. We were standing on the sidewalk. I was having my last cigarette from the Denim Lady.

"OK, here's the plan," I said. "Do whatever you want. How did you find me?"

"I saw the eviction notice. And your stuff was all smashed up, where else would you go?"

"So you found me. And we now have our strategy in place. What else do you want?"

"You still owe me four hundred dollars."

I looked into the vanilla pie of Ninja Pete's face. "I'm going to have to owe you that," I said. "I'm a bit light at the moment."

"There's no Fucko, is there?"

"Only in the laughter of children. See, this is why you shouldn't be doing this kind of thing. You're too dumb for crime."

He gave me hurt little-brother eyes. "But I saved your life! I threw that star right into that guy's arm!"

"Yes, you did. You should retire on that. It was incredible. But you had no idea who those people were."

"But you told me to come! You gave me the go word!"

"You're making my point. You don't know me either. Doing some crazy shit I asked you to do was stupid."

"But . . ." He pantomimed throwing the star.

"Yes. That was good. You were a good ninja that night." A group of men outside the shelter turned their beards our way. "Let's walk."

When he got his voice back two blocks later, it was a whine.

"Why did you hire me anyway?"

"Why did you shoot Lito?"

He clammed up.

"What's the matter, not proud of that?" We passed a square with a lump of art in the middle of it. A couple walked by saying couple things.

"I got away that day."

"Yes, you did get away that day, Ninja Pete. But you were lucky that time, too. Maybe you're too dumb to see that you were cosmically lucky two times in a row. Try to focus. Because there's something else you need to know. Lito didn't do anything to Junko, Ninja Pete."

"I'd prefer you not call me that. And Lito got the drugs. He probably did other things."

"Nope, that was all Clarence. Nobody liked Lito. Why would they involve him? You didn't like him either. You thought he was a shitty little person, a nothing." I blew smoke at him. "But that was you. You're the shitty person. With your little gun. Shooting people."

We walked more. He had no further points to make.

"Where are you going now?" I said.

"I have to go back to work. This is my lunch break."

"I'll walk you there. I wasn't sure what to do about you shooting Lito. After last night I'm ready to call it good. But no more shooting people, Ninja Pete."

"But Paul Dowell . . ."

"You want to shoot him before you stop shooting people?"

He looked away.

"You want to do it for Junko. But you'll get caught and Paul will get away."

"You can't stop me."

"That's true. I'm too tired to even think of a lie for someone as dumb as you. But lay off for a week and I'll get you the four hundred I owe you and two hundred more for your trouble."

"Serious?"

"Let's drink on it." There was a liquor store coming up on the left. "I'll have to owe you this, too." I guided us to a fifth of bourbon. "You can add it to the six hundred."

Back on the sidewalk, I took a swig and passed him the bottle, and he a took a swig and coughed. I smacked him on the back.

"OK, we're done now," I said, putting the bottle in my jacket.

The moorage
of a swan

"THANKS FOR THIS, by the way." I nodded at the double margarita on a crack in the bar at Duke's Chowder Tavern, where Brenda had agreed to meet me. Duke's was a quarter mile from the moorage of her paddleboat swan in the cattails on the west side of What Lake. The place was dozing in the afternoon hours when no one with any sense is in a bar. Brenda was so sharply backlit by the sun from the windows behind her that her face was a black blob.

"Before I forget to tell you, you look like shit," she said.

I didn't get a turn in the shower at the shelter that morning. The bottom edge of my face bandage was crusted with margarita salt.

"Temporary setback."

"You're homeless. You're drunk. Your face is smashed in. You're going to jail."

"Spoken like an amateur. Like a booster of copy toner with no fence."

"You sound like my dad when he was trying to make everyone forget about the damage he did the night before."

"Do you wanna slap me?"

"I don't want to touch your gross bandages."

"Punch me in the stomach?"

"I was thinking pool stick to the solar plexus."

"How about pinching my nipples?"

Her blobby backlit form had been leaning forward but now slumped back down. "You disgust me."

We both drank. "So finish your stupid story," she said.

"That's pretty much it. Except Ninja Pete came to see me at the shelter yesterday."

"That idiot you gave half your money to?"

"That was to keep him on a string until I decided what to do with him."

She sucked an ice cube and spit it back in her glass. "Did you decide?"

"Events overtook us. Anyway, I'm done with him now."

"And your buddies from Dayton?"

"Well, there's the one in jail I already told you about. The main buddy, as it were. The other three . . ."

"Including your lady friend."

"I'm sorry about that. Are you still mad?"

"So mad you weren't able to pass her herpes to me. Talk about something else. How's the shelter?"

"Haven't really made any friends. But I've had time to finish memorizing that poem I was working on when we first met in the coffee shop."

"I have no idea what you're talking about."

"Sure you do. Want to hear some of it?"

"No."

"'And chide the cripple tardy-gaited night who, like a foul and ugly witch, doth limp so tediously—' I wish you wouldn't do that."

She was making the jerk-off motion.

"OK," I said. "One last thing. I promise."

She held up a hand.

"No, not money. I was wondering if you had any ideas about how to track my three friends from Ohio."

"Call Pig Wing."

"Who?"

"If they got back to wherever they're staying, they didn't walk. Pig Wing is the only taxi company in town."

"I knew you'd have an idea. I wouldn't have achieved this level of success without you, I hope you know that."

"What are you going to do when you find them?"

The worst clown
in the world

"ARE YOU A mummy?"

A little boy in front of me was look-ing over his mother's shoulder. I was on the bus to the motel where Rider Pete, Rider Paul, and Lisa were holed up. I'd told Pig Wing I was Plankton PD and could they please tell us about a fare that'd left Packer's Hill around eleven on Friday night. Two white men looking wigged out. They put me on hold and came back and said Sun Sail Inn by the airport.

The bus tooled along into the desert of pavement south of town. A place that looked like they went, "Ah fuck it, who cares about anything out here, shitty motels and jets overhead all day, let's pave the whole fucking thing." It was a shabby crew bussing into that shit zone with me. I felt right at home with my limp and bandages. A career drunk aged between forty and sixty had offered me some of his malt liquor for breakfast at the shelter. It still burned on my breath. It was ten a.m.

"Yes, I'm a mummy. Is your mom single?"

A hand pulled the boy briskly back into his seat.

The Sun Sail Inn's twenty-four hollow-core doors were set in a two-story grin across an acre of black-top. The Riders' car was intelligently parked right in front of the office. I went in. The manager looked up.

"I got a breakfast burrito delivery for the Miller-Sampson-Ridley party."

"Miller-Sampson-Ridley?"

"One of those names. Maybe I wrote it down wrong. Two dudes and a lady."

"Number twenty-two."

"Many thanks."

"Wait, I don't see any delivery."

"Yeah, I gotta phone it in."

I climbed cement stairs to twenty-two on the upper walkway and sat cross-legged beside their door. The shade was drawn over a two-liter plastic bottle of rum on the sill. I couldn't hear anything inside. They were probably exhausted. I was pretty tired myself. I caught a few B-Rays roused out of the clouds by passing airplanes.

Around noon there were low voices and nasty laughter. The door opened and Rider Paul shuffled out in a tank top and sweatpants, holding an ice bucket. He was not happy to see me.

"This motherfucker—! Pete! Come out here!"

Rider Pete erupted out of the door shirtless in his boxers. "Jesus you're loud, what—"

"It's goddamn Pope. You wanna be killed, coming here?"

"Yes, I wanna be killed. Great idea. But how about we go inside? Better to kill in private. Or you could keep screeching and attracting attention."

As usual, they went along because they had no other ideas. I took a seat on the bed. They stood with their arms crossed like bad guys in a movie. The shower was going. Lisa, apparently.

"Banh fucked you up, man. Look at your fucking face." Rider Pete, still shirtless, unfolded his arms to say this and folded them again when he finished.

"Pete, you're looking pretty flabby. Don't get mad, I have the same problem. It's all the booze. Otherwise we'd be cut like a couple of Bruce Lees, right? You white Bruce Lee and me regular Bruce Lee." He had a new tattoo on his bicep. "You know that kanji says *whole cow*, right?"

"It says *power.*"

"Whatever you say. Look, you guys are fucked. Far from home, leader in jail, hunted by the cops . . ."

Pete shuffled in a menacing way, and Paul moved to the door and leaned against it.

"You're confused by my arrival. I get that. But if I was gonna call the cops on you, I'd have done it already."

"Why were you sitting out there like a little weirdo?"

"I wanted to make sure you were awake. If I'd woken you up, you were more likely to do something stupid."

"We might anyway."

"Banh told me you're killers now. Pretty cool. But no one has anything on you. Even if they find you in Ohio, they're not going to send you back here. They've already got Banh. You're just a loose end in a tidy story. They haven't even ID'd your car. You're golden." I had no idea if any of this was true.

Pete rubbed his kanji. "We're not like you. We're not gonna fuck Banh."

"Even if you want to help him, you can't do it here. You want to help, go back and send money."

"We're not taking orders from you, Pope."

"Do what you want. This is solid guidance. Not that I care."

"You've come pretty far out of your way to not care."

"Oh, I didn't come to tell you any of that. I wanna say goodbye to Lisa."

Pete laughed through his nose, and Paul joined in. "She doesn't want to see you."

"If that's true, I'll wish you the best of luck and be on my way. Hey, can I have some of that?" I pointed at the shape the bottle of rum made through the shade.

Rider Pete scoffed and handed me the bottle of rum and a glass. I poured four fingers and nodded toward the shower. "So are either of you, you know …" I held my drink in the crook of my arm and made the fucking gesture. A look passed between them that said they'd both been thinking about it. Two towels entered the room wrapped around Lisa and her hair. She took me in leisurely.

"I thought I heard a party going on out here. Where's *my* drink?"

"How about I buy you a real drink?"

"How about you buy me a real drink? That's pretty good, Suavey Suaverson. What happened to your face?"

"Banh fucked him up, man," said Pete, and he and Paul cackled and high-fived and practically fucked each other in the ass.

I consulted my rum. Its surface was filmed with whatever had been in the glass before. "The Log Cabin Tavern is just down the street."

"It will be hard to tear myself away from these fine stallions, but OK."

Pete made a yipping sound. "You going with this asshole?"

"Gonna tell Banhy on me? Give me ninety seconds, Pope."

Pete and Paul glared and glowered and rebuffed my inquiries into mutual acquaintances until Lisa reappeared in a skirt and sweater, her hair still wet.

"You look like a fresh flower. Was just passing the time with your dads here. I'll have her back by midnight, fellas."

In the parking lot, I waved the bottle of bourbon I'd bagged from Ninja Pete and told her, "I don't actually have any money for that drink, but this is pretty good."

We stopped behind the manager's office. She took the bottle. "You look terrible."

"So I've heard."

She drank. "Not just the bandages and the gimpy walk. The hat. You look like a clown. Like the worst clown in the world."

She tilted the bottle into her face again, but it went down the wrong hole and she doubled over coughing until she snorted bourbon out of her nose. "Oh God, it burns!"

I handed her a shelter-issue napkin from my ass pocket.

"Thanks."

"You're welcome. Give me a cigarette."

"Oh, this is my last one, Popey. I'll share it with you though." She lit it and took a drag and passed it to me.

I said, "So your little vacation is over. What now?"

"I have to go get Junior back from Banh's mom. And find a job? I don't know, what do people do?"

"Did you really give those guys a key to my place?"

"I told you I had to get this thing jump-started. I knew you'd get out of it. And you did!"

"So I get a prize?"

"You want to fuck again?"

I passed the cigarette back to her. "Yes. But that's not what I'm going to ask you for."

"Sure, you'd rather jerk off to your own noble feelings, I get it. So what do you want?"

"Right before the part where he was going to kill me, Banh asked about the money. They think I still have it."

"Don't you?"

"Doesn't matter. They think I do, and I want you to tell them where to find it." I handed her a piece of paper with Paul Dowell's address on it.

"Sure, Pope. I'll do that."

"Tell them not to hurt the cat."

"What?"

"Never mind."

She smoked her cigarette intently. She seemed to be done sharing it with me. "You looked surprised."

"What do you mean?"

"When I said I'd do that for you. Why? Can't you tell I like you?"

The low window

IT'D BEEN THREE weeks since the first time I broke into Frank Boise's office. The plastic bag filled with rain that had sloshed its shadow back and forth was drained and twisted around a branch. Like last time, I pushed a dumpster into place under Boise's window and climbed the lumpy brick wall. This time I tapped on the window.

Boise raised it and pulled me in. "You're a scampering little fuck, aren't you? Like a raccoon."

"I am not a scampering little fuck. I'm a little fuck with a bad foot." Boise didn't believe me when I told him how easy it was to break into his office. "Anyone could do it." He sat down and I took the seat across the desk from him. "Are you going to turn on the lights?"

"Nope."

"How's the poetry going?"

The brim of Boise's hat lifted.

"Are you mad I snooped in your shit?" I said. "Why do you think I broke in?"

He snorted. "Because you're a baby. Babies make messes that adults clean up."

"You're the adult? With all these corpses piling up around you?"

He took his hat off and pointed it at me. "You're lucky not to be dead."

"Are you giving me advice now? Like when you gave me pens and told me not to put my name on cheap crap?"

"I *am* going to give you some advice. If you have a problem with me, knock on the front door like a man and tell me to my face."

"Why? I didn't want to talk to you. You had a con-descending attitude."

"You had a condescending attitude." He did a high-pitched imitation of my voice.

"I don't sound like that."

He rolled his head around and cracked his neck. "I'll give you one thing though."

"Hang on, I want to write this down. Yes?"

"You're good at stirring things up. That's not much. But it's a start. Think about getting a license. An investigator's license."

"I'm pretty sure it was a licensed investigator who threw me in the path of a bunch of murderers."

"You looked like you knew how to run away."

"Maybe in exchange for being such a dick, you could help me out with something. You figure Clarence killed Ed?"

Boise contemplated the splendor of his forearms. "Without a doubt."

"Feel free to go on."

"There's no other way. It wasn't random. Therefore it was someone Ed knew. I know everyone he knew, and no one else could have done it."

"That's pretty thin, Frank."

"Plus, I talked to Clarence when I was working for Mayfern trying to find dirt on Ed to feed the divorce judge, and he as much as admitted it."

"'As much as'?"

"His attitude said it. Preening. He was happy people knew. Like killing someone and dumping them in a bush is a manly accomplishment. Thought he was untouchable."

"That turned out not to be the case."

"He killed someone before, a street person who did some work for him. Ask your buddies at the shelter. They know. You'd know, too, if you knew anything at all about this town."

"Maybe I would if people knew how to have a conversation and not do shit like send me to Yick Fung Overlook. Why *did* you send me to Yick Fung Overlook?"

"I'd lost track of Clarence. I knew you'd talk to Debbie, the lady there. And that she'd mention it to Clarence. I wanted to provoke him into showing himself."

"How did you know I'd talk to her?"

"Who else is there to talk to?"

"Why the envelope, the word 'reindeer'?"

"Clarence would understand. He knew my name used to be Reindeer."

"Reindeer Boise?"

"Frank Reindeer. Changed it for the business. Boise sounds more reliable."

"You're always thinking, Frank."

"You criticize my methods. And yet I'm sitting here and you're sitting there."

"Debbie was nice to me later."

"That means she thinks you're harmless. Now as for your boyfriend, Paul Dowell of TechCo, he'd hired Clarence to do stuff. Back when he thought he was going to leverage his little investment club into drug dealing. Or something. Why a man with a good income would do something so stupid is beyond me."

"It's fun to be bad. Most people aren't good at it."

"Why do you care about Ed's murder anyway?"

"I don't. Just making conversation. I'm here for the thing. Do you have it?"

He slid a jump drive across his desk, tracing the path the red cowboy hat had taken three weeks before. "You really staying at a shelter?" he said.

"The last of my cash went for this. And on second thought, I think you should keep it," I said. "Would the fee I paid cover handing it over to the cops?"

"I thought you didn't like cops."

"I don't. I use cops."

"No, your fee won't cover that. But I'll do it. If you promise to pay for my window when you have money."

"What makes you think I'll have money?"

"You're not cut out for the streets. Way too soft. So you'll figure something out. You know how much an investigator's license costs?"

"Dying to know."

"Fifteen bucks. I might even be able to kick you some work myself."

"Yeah, I'm not real sure I want to pursue further employment with you, Frank."

"Real work. I might need a raccoon sometime."

Flipping the card

"Look at this." I leaned forward in my lawn chair and put a slide on the armrest of Helen's lawn chair.

"Not sure why I let you in."

"Me either. Curiosity? I like what you've done with the place." Besides the two lawn chairs and a car seat, 17 Resentment Court was empty.

"The furniture belonged to the people who lived here before. They finally got around to picking it up. Gives the kid more room to crawl around." The baby stared intently from the car seat. She finally picked up the slide and held it to the light. It showed her with Paul Dowell and company. "Me, at a party. Scary evidence, Skippy."

"It's not where, it's when." The date was dot-matrixed on the back of the slide. "A week after your dad was killed. You must've known by then that these were the people who did it. The only possible reason you could have for going to their party was to get intel. Which I really admire, by the way. I won't pry into what else you did to them. I'm sure they deserved it all."

She looked at some kids across the street. "Saying you were Frank Boise when you first came here was stupid."

"Why talk to me then?"

She turned back to me. Her eyes were very green. "It's nice to be listened to. I liked how you wrote down what I said in your little notebook."

"I guess at some point you gave up on Boise's investigation and decided to start murdering people. But why Lito? Why not Clarence and Paul?"

She smiled. "I was doing them in order of importance. Paul last. So he'd know I was coming."

"And Lito the runt went first."

She stood up. "Let's go outside and smoke."

The baby sighed and mashed his blotchy face against the side of his car seat. We stepped onto her rectangle of brown grass.

"Give me a cigarette," she said.

"I was going to get one from you." I put my fingers to my lips and inhaled.

"What are you doing?"

"Pretending to smoke can fool your system. Try it."

"You're an idiot."

I exhaled invisible smoke at her. "What was Tatsu's role?"

"He didn't have one."

"Why was he after me with an aluminum bat?"

"What does Tatsu know about you except you sneak into his restaurant, harass his employees, and run out on your bill?"

"When you put it like that . . ."

"So are you going to leave now? Or was there something else you wanted?"

"Yeah, I have a question. Did Lito ever miss work?"

"What do you mean?"

"He didn't. He was lazy in a way. Never missed a smoke break in his life. And died owing twenty bucks to everyone he knew. No one liked him. I didn't like him either. But he showed up at every job he had, and he had a bunch of them. Turns out his parents are dead. Sixteen nieces and nephews back in the Philippines. Never missed any of their birthdays." Most of this was made up, but something like it was probably true.

"What do I care?"

"As I explained to the other person who shot Lito that day, Lito wasn't in this. He knew nothing."

"I don't believe you."

"I also need to tell you about a video. I got it on a jump drive. You didn't see the camera in Lito's lobby?"

"Even if you have me going in, so what?"

I followed her back into the house. She adjusted the baby's blanket and flopped into her lawn chair.

"Finally, there's your dad's gun. The beauty of killing his killers with it, how could you resist? And you have two more people to kill." She was frozen on the lawn chair. I was standing. "So I'm guessing it's in this house."

We locked eyes Then she took off for the closet. That was a fake. I slammed against the closet door as she zagged to the bedroom and threw herself on a pillowcase by a mattress on the floor. I came tumbling over her back and wrestled her for it. She locked her jaws on my elbow. I pried her face off me with one hand and her fingers off the gun in the pillowcase with the other. She took some of my flesh with her as she fell in a heap. I took the gun out.

"They'll never convict me."

"Well, you *are* white." I pushed the little lever thing on the gun like Maurice showed me to make the ammo fall out, and put everything back in the pillowcase.

She spit my blood on the floor. "They can't use the gun. No warrant."

"They don't need one. It'll be turned in by a cooperative suspect in a different case involving a late-night ninja attack."

Her hair covered her face. "You're taking away a baby's mother."

"Not me. You did this."

Baby gurgled from the other room. I retrieved my hat from the wreckage of our tussle and paused in the doorway. "You might get what you wanted, by the way. About something bad happening to Paul Dowell. No guarantees. Watch the news though."

Noah, the little boy from unit sixteen, was waiting outside. "Did you kill him?"

"I assume you're referring to our business arrangement regarding Rick Fernmancer. I did not. As you may remember, you gave me five dollars. I did punch him in the face though. You actually got a great deal."

He followed me. "What happened to your arm?"

"The woman in that apartment bit me."

"How much to kill him?"

"I'm getting out of the social worker–killin' business, No. But if you want me to look into this Rick
some more, I can give you a good rate."

"What happened to your face?"

"I mean a *really* good rate. Think you can borrow
some money from your mom's purse?"

"I don't know."

"Try." I handed him a card.

"Your name is Frank Boise?"

"Other side."

The other side said:

Pope Smith
Investigator

"Wait till she's asleep. Call me when you got it," I
said, and rounded the corner.

Thanks

Damon Agnos, Diane Sepanski, Scott Teal,
Molly Watkins, Lilly, Tim Sirotnik,
Scott Kuhlman, and Jessica Blumenthal.
Cover and title page by Marie Bouassi.
Interior design by Andrea Reider.

www.ingramcontent.com/pod-product-compliance
Lightning Source LLC
Chambersburg PA
CBHW070941180726
48291CB00004B/1093